IN THIS TIME

Dave A. Cornelius (Dr. Dave)

JCWALK PUBLISHING

Dr. Dave
Your Thought Partner For Growth

CONTENTS

ACKNOWLEDGEMENTS

Writing this book from the perspective of a black woman protagonist finds influence in my family's matriarch. Alberta Louisa Jenkins (Ma Ruby's), Verni Prunella Yearwood (Ma Vernie), and Celia Elfreda Brow (Ma Celia, when I was little) are the brave women who give me inspiration and vision for life. Their voices travel with me wherever I go.

Minister Sheree Carradine, thank you for your voice of support and encouragement. Your positive energy inspires many.

Keith and Mary Lou Norris, thanks for the guidance on what an RV hookup looks like.

"I can do all things through Christ who strengthens me." Philippians 4:13 NIV
Christ Jesus is at the center of my life, making it possible for me to use the gifts given to me to create and innovate.

FOREWORD

By Minister Sheree Carradine

I was honored to write the foreword to Dr. Dave's book Seven Principles and Habits for Kingdom Living. Each chapter left me in deep thought, stirred my spirit, and filled me with a burning desire to turn the page. Once again, I have the privilege of writing the foreword—this time for In This Time, the third installment of the Ashanti MWendo series.

Dr. Dave has done it again with In This Time, the third installment in the Ashanti MWendo series. Even without reading the previous books, this one stands on its own as a richly layered, thought-provoking work.

At the heart of the book is a powerful metaphor—the soup. Just as a pot of West Indian soup blends unexpected ingredients into one ever-changing experience, life, too, offers a mix we can't control. Sometimes spicy, sometimes savory, the flavors of each moment come together, simmering into the reality we live in. Like time itself, soup is never static. Past, present, and future combine to shape our personal and collective stories.

Cooking, especially making soup, encourages reflection. And this book provides plenty. Through the lives of the MWendo-Joseph family—Ashanti, Ayo, Carmel, and Caleb—we see a beautiful portrait of Black excellence rooted in purpose, love, and leadership. From D.C. to Ghana, their legacy unfolds through innovation, education, and service.

Much like Wakanda redefined how we imagine Black futures, In This Time dares us to dream boldly. It reminds us that our histories are not burdens to carry but launchpads for greatness.

Each page draws us deeper into an Afro-futurist vision where legacy and imagination collide to shape the future.

Prepare to be inspired—and transformed.
Thank you, Dr. Dave, for enlightening us once again. May you continue to let God use you, and may this book reach hearts, stir minds, and inspire lives for generations to come.
— Minister Sheree Carradine

PREFACE

Thinking about the metaphor of 'The Soup,' my mind envisions swirling in a medley of ingredients I do not have control over. There is no way to determine which ingredient will become the prominent flavor. Will carrots, peppercorns, or cloves dominate? It's going to a West Indian soup shop, and I'm unable to control what's in the day's soup. One day is chicken, and the next is pepper pot. Some days are Gungo peas, red peas, seafood, and many other options. There are no à la carte options. You accept what is there and move on. If you refuse to accept the reality of the soups' ingredients and the owner's operating methods, you may experience the Seinfeld episode 'No Soup for You'. In the 'No Soup for You' episode, the soup shop offered the best-tasting soup in the city. People would wait in line just to get a single order. If the customers did not align with the owner's rules, he would say No soup for you and deny them the mouth-watering desires of their heart.

According to the Merriam-Webster dictionary, the 'in the soup' metaphor refers to 'being in a bad situation: in trouble.' Higgs (2023) stated, 'The soup metaphor conveys something deeper and more complex than usual about how our experiences simmer and seep into what feels like our inherent way of being in the world – the amalgamation of all that now just feels like us.' We can also think of the soup metaphor as a design and implementation process for bringing innovations to market.

Cooking is one of my favorite things to do. It creates a space for thought and allows my imagination to run wild about any topic. Making soup is liberating, and the options are limitless. Time, much like a hearty soup, appears to be a continuous, flowing entity, yet it's composed of countless distinct ingredients that give it character and substance. Each ingredient—moments, hours, days—melds together, influencing the overall flavor and texture of our experiences. Sometimes, the soup is thin and flies by in a blur, while other times it's thick with events and seems to stretch on endlessly. We can savor certain spoonfuls, wishing they'd last forever, or find ourselves rushing through less palatable bits. And just as you can't truly separate the carrots from the potatoes once they're simmering, past, present, and future are inextricably linked, each contributing to the rich, complex broth of our lives.

Given the fluidity of "In This Time," the soup metaphor takes on an even deeper resonance. We are, at this very moment, immersed in a specific spoonful of this temporal soup. The flavors we taste, the textures we feel, and the warmth or coolness that permeates our experience are all products of the current ingredients. The choices made by those who prepared the soup before us, the additions we are making, and the subtle changes happening as it simmers, all contribute to "this time." It highlights how each present moment is a unique blend, constantly evolving, and irrevocably linked to what came before and what will follow in the ever-flowing pot of existence.

'In This Time' is the third book in the Ashanti Mwendo fiction series. Ashanti is the CEO of Uwazi. Her husband, Ayo, has become nationally known for his work in STEM education and empowering local communities. Carmel is now college-aged and chose to attend Howard University. Caleb figured he could learn everything he needed to know without going to college.

The story of the Joseph family, hyphenated *as* MWendo-Joseph to honor both heritage and legacy, brings to light a powerful and affirming narrative of an African American family thriving at the intersection of love, learning, and leadership. Far from a singular success story, the MWendo-Josephs exemplify what it means to build a family rooted in purpose and possibility, where STEM is not just a career path, but a language of transformation. From Ayo's role as an educator astronaut to Ashanti's visionary leadership in global tech, and the next-generation brilliance of Carmel and Caleb, their journey offers a compelling portrait of Black excellence in motion. Their impact reverberates from the heart of Washington, D.C., to the communities of Accra, Ghana, where innovation is married with justice, and knowledge becomes a tool for healing, empowerment, and change. Through education, spiritual growth, and digital equity initiatives, the MWendo-Joseph family demonstrates how legacy and leadership can not only coexist but co-create a future in which African American families are no longer the exception in STEM and service; they are the architects of the new norm.

The *Wakanda* movie series, rooted in Marvel's visionary depiction of an unconquered African nation, has become far more than a cinematic spectacle. It is a cultural catalyst. Through its Afro-futurist lens, it reimagines Black identity as inherently brilliant, technologically advanced, spiritually rooted, and globally influential. Wakanda dares descendants of the African diaspora to visualize themselves not through the limitations of colonization or oppression, but through a future shaped by ancestral excellence and boundless innovation. It rewires our cultural imagination, challenging long-held narratives and inviting a new generation to dream expansively, design courageously, and lead unapologetically.

For descendants of enslaved people, a crucial narrative shift—one that reframes their history not as mere survival, but as sovereignty. When legacy acts as a launchpad instead of a burden, it unleashes profound generational power. This reorientation moves beyond simply overcoming, fostering a mindset of ownership over land, language, technology, and vision. Within families, it cultivates new patterns of affirmation and resilience. In communities, it ignites movements for equity and justice. In business, it develops leaders who prioritize purpose alongside profit. *Wakanda* transcends mere escapism; it serves as a blueprint. This book guides us toward an Afro-futurist horizon where memory and imagination converge to forge new futures.

ON THE MOVE AGAIN

Ashanti and Ayo decided it was time for a change and to move back East. Ayo completed the research grant, and the work was published. Ashanti and Ayo partnered and brought entrepreneurship to local communities in Arizona with the help of Uwazi. The desire to work at a historically black college and university (HBCU) was a vision he had with his STEM research work. He also believed an ongoing partnership with Uwazi would be beneficial for the community. A great opportunity awaited Ayo, and Ashanti had the flexibility of working remotely and traveling to the Uwazi offices. As the CEO, she had some flexibility since her responsibilities were promoting her company and scaling Uwazi's capabilities for growth. Caleb and Carmel graduated from high school at 16. Moving was an experience that was normal for the family. Caleb decided he did not need to attend college because he could advance his coding capability by taking online classes and connecting with people in online forums. He asked his parents to invest in his startup business idea instead of covering the costs of four college years.

Caleb's decision did not affect Ashanti and Ayo's dream for their children to go to college because they had confidence in his ability to make good choices. However, Ashanti asked Caleb to be open about her wishes so that he would give the college experience a chance. His response was, Mom, let me live! She knew that his response meant to back off, and she did. Carmel decided to attend Howard University, a Historically Black College and University (HBCU). One of her other college choices included Spelman College in Atlanta, GA. She felt attending a women's liberal arts college would allow her to find sisterhood, a yearning to have a sister as a sibling. However, the family was moving to Washington, D.C., the nation's capital, and Howard University was a good choice. After all, the United States' first female vice president was an alumnus. Many notable alumni attended Howard University. The list was awe-inspiring. Carmel planned to study sustainable design to build suitable structures for the planet. She became a climate change activist and blogged frequently about the need to design sustainable buildings that provided affordable housing. She advocated for designs to support the native people of the United States and around the globe to reflect the cultural designs of their ancestors. The goal was to increase the occupants' health, and the buildings would include modern amenities and fixtures, such as indoor plumbing, central air, air purification, solar and wind, and open-air spaces.

The family wanted to live near Howard University in a neighborhood that supported a family of four and two dogs. A guest room would be ideal to entertain friends and family. A four-bedroom house would be great with an office and a spare dog room. Carmel would live at home and commute to school as an option. The decision to live at home was up to Carmel. Ashanti and Ayo wanted Carmel to learn to make choices on her own. Partnering with twins on the spectrum had been a familiar place for parents and siblings. They knew of the potential challenges and would do anything to protect their children. That's what parents do!

Ayo reflected on the time a cult member tried to convince Carmel to run away from home and join his group. They could intervene and stop her from being manipulated by a predator. That was a scary moment for their family. The kids leaving the family's nest was frightening for Ashanti, Ayo, Carmel, and Caleb. Raising two kids on the spectrum is not easy, and their safety is always a primary concern. There was a private agreement between the couple that Caleb may have been negatively affected by his twin sister's experience. They had to be supportive in every way possible to ensure he knew 'we got you.' The experience with Carmel caused Ashanti and Ayo to lean into their parents' faith, which was a significant shift for science-minded professionals. Despite the challenges, the family remained strong and united, a testament to their resilience and determination.

Ashanti and Ayo found a house near Howard University matching the specifications sent to the realtor. They wanted Carmel to learn to use the Metrorail to commute to school. The public transportation option would also align with Carmie's sustainable goals. Carmel insisted they begin walking the walk to show a commitment to reducing the carbon footprint. How would it look if I were podcasting and blogging about carbon neutrality, and my parents were not doing the right thing? Carmie, moving to an urban community may not allow us to acquire a sustainably designed home, shared Ashanti. Many properties are older, and some buildings' reconstruction uses eco-friendly renewable energy sources. Mom, I know there are options out there. Please stay committed to this journey with me. You are the CEO of Uwazi, a technology company that is committed to carbon neutrality. Caleb said that as long as I can connect to the Internet, it is my primary concern. But I do support Carmie's enthusiastic request. The family's dedication to sustainability, even in the face of challenges, is truly inspiring.

Moving is a pain in the butt, Ayo shouted. We should sell everything and start over with less stuff. That is one way to reduce our carbon footprint. Can we be creative about sustainable living by reducing the number of things we have? There has to be a category for pruning unnecessary stuff. Freeing ourselves of years of keepsakes that we may never look at again, but continue transporting them to our new dwelling places. Caleb, you could create an app that digitizes our stuff in 3D and catalogs the content with some metadata. AI could enhance the capability by telling a story about the content and the owner. We can contextualize the items by inserting the person at the appropriate age interacting with them. Do you mean something like a hologram, Dad? Something like that, Caleb. There are existing apps to inventory and catalog your home, but you want this app to create a visual of the stuff so you can get rid of it. Is that correct, Dad? That's the idea.

Well, Dad, we can have a yard sale and give stuff away to Goodwill and other non-profits that could benefit from our junk. One man's junk is another man's treasure. I wonder where you heard that from, smiled Ayo. Grandpa said Caleb. Yeah, that man is full of sayings from many eras. Living in the Foothills in Tucson was fabulous and may be a retirement option for Ayo and Ashanti. Shortly after going on the market, the realtor sold the house. Selling the house felt permanent. It signaled the move was a reality. Despite the bittersweet feeling of leaving their home, the family remained adaptable and ready to embrace the new chapter in their lives.

THE FAREWELL PARTY

Ashanti and Ayo planned a party to say goodbye to colleagues and friends. They also wanted to create time and space for Caleb and Carmel to connect with local friends in the Tucson community. The time spent there allowed many relationships to develop and remain in the future. Especially the people we met in the Jack and Jill community. The friendships cultivated were meaningful for our survival in the early days of living in a university community. Ayo, I know you are going to invite your university friends. Doug is a sure invite; that goes without saying, babe. He was one of my early friendships as a visiting professor. I am going to miss the people here. But the good news is we will maintain a condominium here, so we can always visit. We are blessed to be in this position, Shanti. We have to find a theme for the party. It cannot be a traditional goodbye party. Mom and Dad, can we have a photo booth and karaoke stage with a large screen and sound system? Carmel suggested we could have a scavenger hunt to discover items we should give away, Dad. Caleb smirked at the idea.

Ashanti agreed and said we should organize and develop ideas to make this an event. I like your thinking, babe. The siblings had debated for days over the perfect theme. They created a group chat to engage their friends in planning the party. Their first order of business was to develop a theme and a name for the party. After much deliberation, they settled on "The Odyssey" to signify the exciting new chapters ahead for their friends and family. The theme was a nod to the future and celebrated their shared adventures. The party theme and name idea were from Star Trek Discovery with Michael Burnham, their favorite series. Caleb said, "I want to start with a tug-of-war to engage people actively." The tug-of-war area would have a slip-and-slide with a mud pool. I can't wait to see how people navigate that challenge. This party is going to be epic. Carmie added, "The Photo Booth before and after would be crazy to show what our friends looked like before and after."

We should follow that activity with a water balloon hide-and-seek blended game, yelled Carmie. Can you visualize the chaos and excitement of being found and blasted with water balloons? When did you come up with that idea? As we planned the party, combining different aspects of the fun games we played before would be great. Gotta give it to us—ideas from the minds of twins.

THE ODYSSEY PARTY

The day of the party was upon the family, and the twins couldn't wait to see friends for a blast of a time. Caleb and Carmel stood on the porch of their home, scanning the backyard as a kaleidoscope of colors began to take shape. Banners, streamers, and balloons in vibrant hues decorated the trees, and tables displayed an array of snacks and drinks. It was the perfect setting for the going-away party they had planned for weeks. Alright, Carmel, Caleb said, a mischievous twinkle in his eye. It's time to gamify this party and make it unforgettable. As guests arrived, Caleb and Carmel greeted them with customized adventure badges. Each badge had a unique symbol representing elements like fire, water, earth, and air, signifying the attendees' diverse experiences and personalities. Ashanti and Ayo took a back seat to Carmel and Caleb, giving them the freedom to be the master of ceremony (MC) and Toastmaster for the event.

SLIP-AND-SLIDE TUG-OF-WAR WITH A MUD POOL

Welcome, adventurers! Carmel announced, her voice carrying over the buzz of conversation. Today, we're embarking on one final journey together. To make it memorable, we have games and activities to test your skills, creativity, and teamwork. Let the games begin! The first game is the Slip-and-Slide Tug-of-War with a Mud Pool. Caleb, would you tell our friends how to play the game?

Team Formation: Divide the guests into two teams. Each team lines up on opposite ends of the slip-and-slide, gripping the rope tightly.

Objective: The goal is to pull the opposing team across the slip-and-slide and into the mud pool. The team that pulls the other team into the mud pool first wins.

Safety Precautions: Participants should wear old clothes or swimsuits that they don't mind getting muddy. Everyone should wear sneakers or water shoes to avoid slipping. A few spotters are placed around the area to ensure no one gets hurt and to help anyone who might need assistance getting out of the mud pool.

Starting Signal: A whistle or loud shout signals the start of the game. Teams pull the rope with all their might, trying to gain traction on the slippery surface.

Action: As the teams pull, participants slide and struggle to maintain their footing on the slick plastic. The slip-and-slide adds an element of chaos and fun as players slip, slide, and laugh while trying to stay upright.

Victory: The team that successfully pulls the opposing team into the mud pool is declared the winner. Cheers and laughter erupt as the losing team splashes into the muddy water.

Clean-Up: A garden hose or a small inflatable pool filled with clean water is nearby for participants to rinse the mud. Use the towels to help everyone clean up and dry off.

Photos: A designated photo area with props and a backdrop allows for muddy team photos. We can capture the fun and messy moments, creating lasting memories for everyone.

Awards: The winning team will receive small prizes or ribbons; all participants receive a token for their enthusiasm and sportsmanship.

The Slip-and-Slide Tug-of-War with a Mud Pool will surely be a highlight of the party, providing laughter, excitement, and unforgettable fun for all ages.

Carmie, would you tell our friends how to play the Water Balloon Hide-and-Seek game?

WATER BALLOON HIDE-AND-SEEK BLENDED GAME

The Water Balloon Hide-and-Seek Blended Game combines the strategic elements of hide-and-seek with the fun and refreshing aspect of water balloon fights, ensuring an exciting and memorable experience for all participants.

Location: The game setup will be in the backyard with plenty of hiding spots. Trees, bushes, and other outdoor structures provide ideal places for participants to hide.

Water Balloons: Hundreds of water balloons are filled and placed in large buckets or containers around the play area. Additional water balloon stations are available strategically to ensure a steady supply.

Safe Zones: Designate a few "safe zones" where hiders can temporarily be free from being blasted. These could be marked areas or objects like a large tree or patio.

Team Formation: Divide the players into groups of Seekers and Hikers. The Seekers start at a designated place, while the Hikers use a 10-second countdown to find a hiding spot.

The objective for Hiders: Stay hidden as long as possible without being found and blasted by water balloons.

The objective for Seekers: Find and blast all the Hiders with water balloons.

Alternative Rule for Seekers: If a Seeker passes by a hiding spot without discovering the person hiding there, the Hider can blast the Seeker with a water balloon.

Countdown: The game begins with a countdown. Hiders have 2 minutes to find a hiding spot while the Seekers stay at the base with their eyes closed or covered.

Seekers' Search: After the countdown, Seekers begin searching for the Hiders, carrying buckets of water balloons.

Hiders' Defense: Hiders try to remain hidden and can blast Seekers with water balloons if the Seekers get too close to their hiding spot without noticing them.

Blasting: When a Seeker finds a Hider, they must blast them with a water balloon to count them as "found." Once found and blasted, Hiders can join the Seekers or go to a designated area to wait until the game ends.

Safe Zones: Hiders can move between hiding spots and safe zones, but must be careful not to be seen. Safe zones offer temporary protection for Hiders and water blasting.

Victory Conditions: The game continues until all Hiders are found and blasted. The last Hider found can be declared the winner, or the team of Seekers can be declared winners if they see all Hiders within a set time limit.

Refill and Restart: Refill the water balloons and start a new round, switching the roles of Seekers and Hiders to keep the game fresh and exciting.

Awards: Give small prizes or certificates for the best hiders, the most effective Seekers, and the player with the best aim.

Group Photo: Take a group photo with everyone soaking wet and smiling, capturing the fun and excitement of the game.

Refreshments: Have cool drinks and snacks ready for everyone to enjoy and rehydrate after the game.

TREASURE HUNT GAME

Caleb organized a treasure hunt that spanned the entire backyard. Clues were hidden in various locations, each leading to the next with riddles and puzzles to solve. The final treasure was a chest filled with small keepsakes and mementos for the guests to take home.

Memory Lane Trivia: Carmel orchestrated a trivia game centered around memorable moments from their shared past. Questions ranged from funny incidents to significant milestones, ensuring everyone had a chance to reminisce and laugh together.

Adventure Challenges: Various stations were available where guests could participate in mini-challenges. From a mini obstacle course to a creative photo booth where they could dress up and take pictures, each activity encouraged fun and engagement.

Message in a Bottle: Caleb set up a station with parchment paper and pens where guests could write heartfelt messages or advice for the future. A decorative bottle was available to place the message as a cherished keepsake.

THE ODYSSEY PARTY FAREWELL

As the sun began to set, casting a golden glow over the yard, Carmel gathered everyone for the farewell ceremony. Caleb unfurled a large map and posted it on the back of a ping pong table. Each guest could pin their current location and future destinations, symbolizing the journeys they were about to embark on. Before we say see you again soon, Carmel began, her voice tinged with emotion. Let's take a moment to appreciate the adventures we've shared and the memories we've made. Though our paths may diverge, our forged bonds will remain strong. The evening culminated in a heartfelt farewell, during which each guest had the opportunity to say a few words. Tears, laughter, and hugs followed as stories were shared and gratitude expressed. Caleb and Carmel handed out sparklers to signify the end of the party and the beginning of new adventures. Everyone lit their sparklers and stood together in a circle, creating a shimmering, glowing light ring. To new adventures and lasting memories! Caleb shouted, raising his sparkler high. The group echoed his sentiment, their voices blending into the night as the sparklers flickered out, leaving a sense of warmth and unity lingering in the air. As the last guests departed, Caleb and Carmel stood on the porch with Ashanti and Ayo, surveying the quiet yard. We did it, Caleb said, a satisfied smile on his face. Carmel nodded, leaning her head on his shoulder. We did. And it was perfect. In that moment, they knew that no matter where their paths might lead, the memories of this night would stay with them, a testament to the power of friendship and the promise of future adventures.

DRIVING ACROSS THE COUNTRY TO WASHINGTON, DC.

The morning to leave came faster than expected. Time waits for no one. Everyone was running around packing last-minute things. It's time to get going. Dad, why can't we just fly there? It will be a six-hour red-eye flight, and we will be there tomorrow morning. Caleb, where is the fun in that? We get to experience the country traveling from the Southwest to the Mid-Atlantic, but some still think of Washington, DC, as the South. It will take four to five days. We start in Tucson, AZ, and go to Texas, New Mexico, Tennessee, Virginia, and Washington, DC. It is about 2,301 miles total. If we drive 288 miles, each segment will last roughly 4 hours and 30 minutes. We could do about three segments for 12 hours daily. We each could drive two-hour shifts and share the burden. Also, the driver gets to choose the music for their two hours. Think about the adventures and stories you can journal and share with your future kids one day. Really, Dad! We are just 16 years old.

Hey, I grew up on an island, so there was not much cross-country driving when I was growing up. Ayo was born and raised in Antigua and Barbuda. He excelled academically, earning a scholarship to study abroad in the United Kingdom (UK), where he further honed his skills and knowledge in science and technology. Consider visiting the Alamo in San Antonio, Texas, and strolling along the River Walk. Arkansas has many historic civil rights stories. There is a rich music scene in Nashville, Tennessee. Boxing great Muhammad Ali came from Louisville, Kentucky. Richmond, Virginia, has historic sites and stories to help us learn more about our country. Scholars Booker T. Washington and George Washington, the United States' first president, share Virginia roots. Dad, were Booker T. and President George related? Ah, that's another conversation during our drive across the country. Finally, we will visit the Martin Luther King, Jr. monument in Washington, D.C., and the other is to expand our knowledge. Here is the driving schedule. I will take the first segment, then Carmie, followed by Ashanti, and close the second segment with Caleb.

It is 7 A.M., and it is time to get on the road. Let's go, let's go! We need to get Uno and Duos ready for the trip. Lord knows how excited Uno can be when he sees so many people leaving the house at the same time. Uno and Duos are the recent additions to the family—two Beagles rescued from the animal shelter. Is everyone in the Remote vehicle (RV)? The engine is running, and it's time to hit the road. Let's go, let's go! Babe, you are too excited to drive this giant mobile home. Kids, do you agree, asked Ashanti. Yes, Dad wants to be a cowboy in an RV. Gitty-up laughed, Ayo!

Ashanti said calmly, I look forward to seeing the different parts of the country, but I am looking forward to seeing Kathy Smith in Virginia. She has been such a solid friend and mentor. I can testify to that, Ayo shaking his head in agreement. Kathy is family! She always wants us to call her Nana, said Carmie. She never had kids, and you and Caleb have been the closest relationship for her to have grandchildren, responded Ashanti. I have the best music playlist to get us started, interrupted Caleb, and it is a mix of oldies for Dad and fresh stuff for Carmie and me. What about me, Ashanti said, looking over her shoulder. Mom, you have the same taste as Dad. That's not true, she protested. Your Dad likes punk rock and those YellowMan raps. Not my taste, she said with a grimace on her face. Duos whimpered as if to indicate that she agreed with Ashanti.

The drive from Tucson, AZ, to San Antonio, TX, is about 875 miles, roughly 12.5 hours on the I-10E highway. Calculating to drive 293 miles (four hours) per segment would result in more than three segments. We will drive from Tucson, AZ, for 293 miles over four hours, with our first stop being Vado, NM. The second segment will be four hours and will run 293 miles to Fort Stockton, TX. The third segment is 291 miles to San Antonio, TX, for four hours. The first overnight stay will be at the San Antonio / Alamo KOA Holiday in San Antonio. We will arrive around 9:00 PM Central Standard Time (CST), just in time to get dinner, shower, and hit the sack early.

The drive began with enthusiasm, as this was a novel experience for the family. The RV stereo played his favorite music since it was Ayo's turn to drive. The first song was Yellowman, 'Zung-gu-zung gu-gu zung-gu-zeng.' Dad, what is he saying? Who is Yellowman? Carmie Yellowman was one of the first island DJs and rappers from Jamaica. He got his name because of his albinism, a genetic disorder of partial or complete lack of melanin in the skin, hair, and eyes. People would bully him for his looks. Dad, are people harmed in Africa because of albinism? I searched the Internet and found several results from the United Nations discussing the topic of people with albinism being targeted, attacked, and killed. That's sad but true, replied Ayo.

As the family leaves Tucson, they encounter vast expanses of the Sonoran Desert, punctuated with iconic saguaros, golden sands, and rugged mountains in the distance.

As the morning heat increased, shimmering heat waves danced on the horizon. Ayo thought I did not realize how similar the landscape would be as they traveled on the I-10. Everything looked the same, and I could easily fall asleep. A big wheel truck passed by and moved the RV a bit, causing Ayo to snap out of his trance and focus on driving. I need to pay attention to protecting the family's safety on this cross-country drive.

Carmie drove the second two hours of the first segment. Her first song was 'Golden' by Jill Scott. Ashanti yelped and said, Child, where did you get this old soul from? Mom, you played this song when I was in your womb and while I was a baby in my crib. What do you expect? Caleb chuckled and said, Dad, I'm so excited that you didn't play Yellowman for me during my birthing years and when I was a babe. That would never happen, said Ashanti. I am not a fan. They all laughed out loud.

The desert gives way to rocky mesas and the Organ Mountains. The family drives through rolling plains with low shrubs and scattered yucca plants, entering New Mexico. Fields of pecan trees near Las Cruces offer a surprise green oasis amidst the arid backdrop. The Rio Grande River occasionally peeks into view. The first driving segment ended in Vado, NM, and it was time to switch to the Ashanti and Caleb pairing for the second segment. Let's get out, stretch our legs, and allow Uno and Duos to do their business and run for a few minutes. It was time for lunch. The family packed a lunch and was ready for an outdoor picnic beside the RV. The family's food preferences ranged from pescatarian (Carmie) to vegan (Ashanti), pesce-pollotarians (Ayo), and a mix of all of the above (Caleb). The drinks included an island favorite of non-alcoholic ginger beer and Saril. The dogs got a treat as it was lunchtime and fed twice daily.

It's time to hit the road. Let's go! It was Ashnti's turn to start the second segment, and she was ready to go. Ashanti's music taste was very Motown flavored and started with Aretha Franklin's 'Respect' song. The whole family sang and danced to Aretha's famous song. There was an unexpected shift in energy as the lunch effect sank in, and the entire family, including Uno and Duos, went to sleep. Ashanti left to her thoughts for the next hour. Ayo woke up and said, You're supposed to be awake with your mom as the co-pilot, Caleb. Sorry, Dad, I couldn't stay awake to Mom's soft music. It was too mellow after lunch. They made the scheduled stop for a two-hour segment change so Caleb could drive the final hours of the second segment to Fort Stockton, TX. Caleb started his first song with a roar, a throwback to Cult of Personality by the band Living Colour. He needed crunchy music to keep him awake during the drive. Mom, Dad, were you living in New York City when this band was popular? Caleb asked. We were probably there at the time, but we were not big fans. Given your musical taste, I can understand your indifference to that style of music based on your Motown and Dancehall preferences.

Carmie woke up a half-hour into Caleb's driving shift and asked where we were. Caleb responded and said we are going to Fort Stockton, TX. As they cross into Texas, the landscape gradually flattens out, with more shrubs and grasslands, eventually giving way to the Texas Hill Country with its gentle slopes and rocky outcrops. This stretch felt endless, with flatlands gradually becoming more rugged as the RV pushed east. Oil pumps and wind farms break up the vast emptiness. Open skies dominated the landscape as sunsets painted the plains in fiery reds and oranges. Night came, and darkness prevailed; starry nights offered a glimpse of the Milky Way in unpolluted skies. Six hours passed, and the unfamiliar experience of driving in an RV was taking effect. The second segment was much quieter than expected. The Fort Stockton, TX stop was a quick turnaround lasting only

30 minutes. Carmie, make sure Uno and Duos go to the bathroom, shouted Asanti. Got it, Mom!

THE LAST SEGMENT TO SAN ANTONIO

Ayo instructed Carmie to drive for the first two hours, and he would drive the final two hours into San Antonio. The change-over from Carmie to Ayo for the drive into San Antonio was a quick stop. Ayo asked if anyone needed to go outside the RV. We are good, Dad. Let's keep moving. As they approached San Antonio, the landscape began to soften. Rolling hills, lush green pastures, and oak trees signal the transition to the Hill Country. Hey everyone, we will spend the night at an RV park. Tomorrow, we will spend the day at the Riverwalk and the Alamo. As they approached San Antonio on I-10, the city slowly revealed itself. The first signs of the town are the typical markers of a large urban area: housing developments, shopping centers, and industrial parks gradually become more frequent. Caleb and Carmie began noticing the highway widening, with more lanes and exits appearing. The closer the RV got to the city center, the taller the buildings grew. The scenery shifts again after leaving the highway and heading toward the chosen RV park. Tree-lined streets with residential neighborhoods, followed by roads with a rural feel. Hey everyone, watch for signs directing us to the RV park. It is pretty dark out here.

Finally, the RV park was in sight, and they drove toward the reserved parking slot. An attendant came over to help Ayo and Caleb connect the water, waste, electrical, and fuel lines. What is your name, Ayo asked the service attendant. I am Roger. Ayo responded in kind, I am Ayo. Caleb looked down and said it was a pleasure to meet you, Roger. I am Caleb. Hey, said Roger! Roger looked at Ayo and asked, have you ever parked one of these beasts in a tight spot? My first time, Ayo laughed. We had trouble just putting gas into this thing. Roger smiled. Well, I am here to get you parked and settled for tonight. Shanti and Carmie, please come out of the RV and bring Uno and Duos with you. This parking experience could be a topic of discussion by our family for many years. Ashanti and Carmel got the dogs and moved out of the way with cameras ready to capture the epic moment of Ayo parking the RV.

PARKING THE RV

Roger said parking and connecting an RV to utilities can be moderately challenging and tricky, depending on the RV. I will be your spotter to get you into your assigned parking spot. You are lucky to have a backup camera system on this rig. Your mirrors will also help guide you. I need to review a series of hand signals I will provide as your spotter. Caleb, can you capture these instructions with your camera, asked Ayo. It will be helpful in the future when you are parking the RV. Caleb's face changed as he considered parking the beast. Roger began the instructions by asking Caleb, are you ready? Caleb said, go for it! Please follow these instructions:

- Arms crossed in an X pattern or a single closed fist = STOP
- One arm pointing straight to one side or the other = GO RIGHT or GO LEFT
- Arms parallel and moving toward and away from the driver = STRAIGHT BACK
- Arms bent at elbows, hands moving closer together or fur-

ther apart = DISTANCE TO GO
- Arms bent at elbows, palms down, hands motioning down-ward = SLOW DOWN
- Circles with finger to left or right = CUT WHEEL LEFT/RIGHT

Ayo took a few attempts to get used to the hand signals. The Go Right and Go Left signals posed a challenge for him when parking the RV. After a few attempts, Ayo could park the RV in the assigned space. Well, a few times, it took over ten minutes. Roger offered to connect the water, waste, electrical, and fuel lines. Without hesitation, Ayo said, Yes, please. Caleb, Carmel, and Ashanti laughed and said, you had better pay the man for saving us tonight. Ayo gave Roger $20 as a tip for connecting the necessary lines to the RV and for his support as a spotter.

SAN ANTONIO, TEXAS

Okay, family. We are bunking here tonight and will get up at 7:00 AM tomorrow. It is 8:00 PM CST, and I am ready to hit the sack. If anyone wants to shower, they can do so inside the RV. Your mom and I will take the dogs for a short walk and get them to use the bathroom. Dad, don't we need to feed them first and then take them out? What about feeding us? We didn't have dinner either. That's right! I am a little off with this RV living that started today. Dad, Caleb may have been on to something about that red-eye flight, smirked Carmie. There was silence. Babe, are we spending an extra day here to visit the sites in San Antonio? It is the only way to stay on the 12-hour drive cycle of three four-hour segments. Ayo said, I guess that is our reality, isn't it? Ashanti chuckled. As they say, no one plans to fail, but we indeed fail to plan. Ayo slapped back and said, there is no failure, just learning. We have limited experiments and learn as we go to make the best choices. The family finally settled down at 10:00 PM and fell into a deep sleep. Even the dogs were snoring.

7:00 AM came faster than expected. Driving 12 hours was challenging, and it was the first experience for Ashanti, Ayo, the kids, and the dogs to travel across the country. Ayo was first up and began getting breakfast ready for his family. He pulled out his phone to get oriented with his family's eating habits. The family's food tastes ranged from pescatarian (Carmie) to vegan (Ashanti), pesce-pollotarians (Ayo), and all of the above (Caleb). He started by feeding the dogs and getting them ready to go outside. He fired up the gas grill, then connected the Foodi to toast the bagels. They all enjoyed eggs, so that was an easy choice to make. He started banging pots and pans to wake the family. Rise and shine, he yelled. Rise and shine! Come on, Dad! Why are you doing this? It felt like I had not even slept yet. I am so tired, complained Caleb. Alright, Ayo, we hear you. Ashanti got up and kissed him. Do you want me to take the dogs outside to do their business? That would be great, and I can get breakfast ready for us. Carmel walked down the hall into the bathroom and started her morning routine to get ready. Caleb jumped up, ran to the bathroom, and started pounding on the door. Carmel, I need to go! I need to go badly. She yelled back, dude, I'm using the bathroom. Ayo noticed the noise and yelled, Caleb, use the bathrooms at the RV campground. Caleb started ambling toward the RV door and gently walked to the public bathrooms at the park. On returning to the RV, he ran into Ashanti, Uno, and Duos and walked into the park. Do you feel better now? What? What are you talking about? Your dad texted me and informed me that you may not make it to the bathroom, so be on the lookout. That's not funny, mom. Ashanti leaned in and gave him a hug and a kiss.

They finished breakfast, and it was time to clean up and prepare for the day in San Antonio. We will use a ride-share service to visit the Alamo and the Riverwalk. Uno and Duos can enjoy the experience with us without being left alone. The rules for Alamo visitors say Uno and Duos cannot enter the buildings or grounds. Okay, then, that changes the priority. The plan is to visit the Riverwalk with the dogs and enjoy the 15-mile-long trail. Also, there is a public park nearby to visit with the dogs. Uno may find new dog butts to sniff at the park. I wonder why he does that, Carmie pondered aloud. According to the Internet, they sniff each other's bum to identify if they have met before because of the unique scent of each dog, said Caleb. We humans do not understand why dogs do what they do. We may need to bring blankets for them to lie on since it will be a hot mid-July day in Texas. Do we have the dog's booties? Let's get their bowls and water. That should give us the flexibility to handle our pets and the weather. If we want to see the Alamo, it's just a few blocks away, and we can decide if it's a place we'd like to visit with our family and dogs.

The quad arrived at the San Antonio Riverwalk with the dogs and visited a Mexican restaurant for lunch on the river. The Riverwalk will be easier since dog accommodations are available on the boardwalk. The kids can also go on boat rides, just as long as they are on a leash. The kids spoke fluent Spanish and began to have a conversation with the server.

Servidor: ¡Hola! Bienvenidos a nuestro restaurante. ¿Es su primera vez aquí en San Antonio?
Server: Hello! Welcome to our restaurant. Is this your first time in San Antonio?

Carmel: ¡Sí! Es nuestra primera vez aquí. Nos dijeron que este lugar es famoso. ¿Qué es lo más rico del menú?
Carmel: Yes! It's our first time here. We heard this place is famous. What's the best thing on the menu?

Servidor: Bueno, tenemos muchas opciones deliciosas. Si les gusta algo auténtico, les recomiendo los tacos al pastor o el mole poblano. Para algo más suave, las enchiladas de queso son muy populares con los niños. ¿Qué les gustaría probar?
Server: Well, we have many delicious options. If you like

something authentic, I recommend the *tacos al pastor* or *mole poblano*. For something milder, the cheese enchiladas are very popular with kids. What would you like to try?

Caleb: Hmm... Los tacos al pastor suenan bien. ¿Son muy picantes?
Caleb: Hmm... The *tacos al pastor* sounds good. Are they very spicy?

Servidor: No mucho, pero si prefieren algo más suave, podemos hacerlos sin salsa picante. ¿Qué les parece?
Server: Not too much, but if you prefer something milder, we can make them without spicy sauce. How does that sound?

Carmel: ¡Perfecto! Yo quiero enchiladas, pero sin cebolla. ¿Eso es posible?
Carmel: Perfect! I want enchiladas, but without onions. Is that possible?

Servidor: Claro que sí. Podemos prepararlas como les guste.
Server: Of course! We can prepare them just the way you like.

Ayo and Ashanti interrupted and spoke in English. Can we get our orders in as well? Yes sir. What would you like? We will both have the chicken enchiladas with green sauce and a beer.

Servidor: Ahora, cambiando un poco de tema, ¿están explorando la ciudad?
Server: Now, changing the subject a little, are you exploring the city?

Caleb: Sí, queremos hacer un paseo en el río. ¿Cuál es el mejor tour?
Caleb: Yes, we want to take a river ride. Which is the best tour?

Servidor: Les recomiendo el **Go Rio River Cruise**. Es muy divertido y les cuentan muchas historias interesantes sobre la ciudad. Además, las vistas desde el río son hermosas.

Server: I recommend the **Go Rio River Cruise**. It's very fun, and they tell many interesting stories about the city. Plus, the views from the river are beautiful.

Carmel: ¡Suena increíble! ¿Cuánto tiempo dura?
Carmel: That sounds amazing! How long does it last?

Servidor: Aproximadamente 35 minutos. Es perfecto para ver lo más importante del Riverwalk sin cansarse.
Server: About 35 minutes. It's perfect to see the highlights of the Riverwalk without getting too tired.

Caleb: También tenemos a nuestro perrito con nosotros. ¿Hay algún parque cerca que sea seguro para los perros y visitantes?
Caleb: We also have our dog with us. Is there a park nearby that's safe for dogs and visitors?

Servidor: Sí, el parque más cercano es **Hemisfair Park**. Es un lugar muy bonito y seguro, con áreas específicas para perros. También tiene espacio para caminar y jugar, así que creo que les encantará.
Server: Yes, the closest park is **Hemisfair Park**. It's a very nice and safe place, with specific areas for dogs and space for walking and playing, so I think you'll love it.

Carmel: ¡Gracias por la recomendación! ¿Es fácil llegar allí desde aquí?
Carmel: Thanks for the recommendation! Is it easy to get there from here?

Servidor: Muy fácil. Está a solo unos 10 minutos caminando desde el Riverwalk. Pueden pedir indicaciones si necesitan.
** Server **: It's very easy. It's about a 10-minute walk from the Riverwalk. If you need directions, ask.

Caleb: ¡Gracias! Creo que ya sabemos qué hacer después de comer.

Caleb: Thanks! I think we know what to do after eating.

Servidor: Me alegra escuchar eso. Ahora, voy a preparar su orden. Si necesitan algo más, no duden en llamarme. ¡Disfruten su tiempo en San Antonio!
Server: I'm glad to hear that. Now, I'll prepare your order. If you need anything else, don't hesitate to call me. Enjoy your time in San Antonio!

The family ate in silence for an hour. Carmel dropped some food for Uno and Duos on the floor. Carmie, you know feeding the dogs our food is bad for them. Caleb looked at her with a protesting look. We are on vacation, and so are they. Carmie placed her hands under her chin and smiled.

Ayo looked at Shanti and asked, "Are you with us? Your head seems to be elsewhere. Are you daydreaming?" I am thinking about Kathy. She has been on my mind all day today. You know how I get when my brain belly starts acting up.
I look forward to seeing her in person. It has been two years since she retired and moved to Virginia. The good news is we will see her in a few days, Ayo said empathetically.
Ashanti snapped out of her self-reflective mood and said, We should go to the park first, then get on the river boats. This way, we can get Uno and Duos to let out some energy. We would work off some calories after that big lunch. That's a good idea, said Carmel. I would hate to fall asleep while we were on the river-boat. Who knows, one of us could fall into that beautiful, clear water.

After about an hour in Hemisfair Park, they felt the dogs had gotten enough exercise, and they got to take a digestion walk. The family returned to the Riverwalk and got on the recommended Go Rio River Cruise. The knowledgeable guides began sharing engaging stories and historical insights about the city's landmarks and heritage as they glided along the San Antonio River. The first site was La Villita, which holds historical significance as the location where General Santa Anna positioned his cannon line during the Battle of the Alamo. The next interesting place was Selena's Bridge. A picturesque spot on the river, this bridge gained fame as the location where Tejano superstar Selena Quintanilla-Pérez's husband proposed to her in the movie, making it a romantic and culturally significant landmark. Throughout the cruise, the guides shared the diverse cultural influences that have shaped San Antonio, including German, Mexican, French, Irish, and American Indian heritages. This blend of cultures creates a unique, vibrant, distinctly San Antonio atmosphere. The family walked to an area with chairs and a covering at the end of the Riverwalk boat tour. Mom, would you like to visit the Alamo with me? Indeed, smiled Ashanti. Wow, that almost sounded like a date, Shanti. Are you jealous? She responded.

Ayo and Carmie stayed with the dogs in shaded areas on the Riverwalk. Ashanti and Caleb began the tour on the Alamo Plaza to get oriented to what the Alamo would look like back in 1836. Lines and plaques indicate the fort's design in 1836. The Alamo historic sites, now squeezed between the bustling city of San Antonio, eleven plaques, and modern statues denoting previous buildings. The long barracks and the Spanish Mission church are the only remaining buildings from 1836. The tour lasted about 45 minutes, and they walked back to meet up with Ayo and Carmel. Uno and Duos were sleeping when they arrived. How was it, Ayo? Visiting the Alamo was overwhelming because there were so many people everywhere, shared Caleb. Carmie said, Dad, I don't want to go to the Alamo. I can watch a YouTube video and get all the information I need about the Alamo. I can get a virtual tour using the new VR headset when we return to the RV. OK, family, are we ready to head back to the RV? Everyone got up, including the dogs. I will take that as a sign that we are leaving. Let me call for a ride back to the park.

After arriving at the RV camp, Ayo and Caleb decided to grill veggie burgers, turkey burgers, and corn for dinner. Ashanti and Carmel went inside the RV with Uno and Duos. Carmel grabbed the VR headset and watched the Alamo tour and reenactment of the war. Ladies, yelled Ayo. Dinner is ready. Caleb grabbed the travel chairs and placed them in a circle. These chairs had a fold-out table attached to place plates, utensils, and cups for eating. Ashanti and Carmel came outside with the dogs and sat on the picnic chairs. During dinner, Ayo asked the family what they had learned from our adventures that day. Dad, you are such an educator. Can we just sit and eat dinner? Carmie, baby, this is how we learn from each other. Carmie got up and went into the RV to grab the Backgammon boards. She returned with a declaration that she would beat everyone soundly and that we would have fun.

The following day, Ayo was up at 6:00 AM, but this time, Ashanti joined him to prepare breakfast for the family. Honey, you are taking the dogs out this morning. I did it yesterday. That's not a problem, babe. I got this. This time, Caleb got to the bathroom before Carmel. He was hogging the bathroom. Carmel said, Fine, I'll go to the public bathroom; I don't mind. Ashanti said, not without an escort, you won't. Ashanti texted Ayo, then called and asked him to walk with Carmel to the bathroom. Dad, this feels like when I was a little girl. You went with me to the bathroom and stepped inside to ensure things were safe. That's my job as your Dad, Carmie. When she finished using the bathroom, they returned to the RV together.

Ashanti kissed Ayo when he came into the RV and said, "You are such a great protector of our family. I chose the best partner ever. " He took a deep breath and fought back the tears. "Are you trying to make me cry, babe? " No, I just felt it was important to share that thought and feeling with you. OK, let's eat breakfast and hit the road. Your mom is trying to make me cry. Here are the details for the drive to Nashville, TN. The trip is 939 miles, with an estimated drive time of 13:41 hours. It will consist of four segments of 235 miles, each lasting 3.5 hours. The first segment is from San Antonio to Italy, TX, 235 miles for 3:24 hours. The second segment is from Italy, TX, to Texarkana, AR, which is 235 for 3:17 hours. The third segment is from Texarkana, AR, to Heth, AR, and is 235 miles for 3:35 hours. The fourth and last stop of the day is Nashville, TN, which is 234 miles away, for 3:33.

Ashanti will take the first segment, the second by Caleb, the third by Carmie, and I will take us into Nashville. If we are on the road by 7:00 AM, the estimated arrival time will be 8:30 PM. The good news: San Antonio and Nashville are in the same time zone. Wait a minute, Dad. You said we would each drive two-hour segments. Now, you have changed things to three-and-a-half-hour segments. What is that all about? I know what the original plan was, Carmie, but that way we could get there without spending another day on the road. Also, we can stop every two hours if necessary. Is everyone OK with the new plan? Let's go for it and see what happens, agreed Caleb. We are good, said Shanti. Well, it is a plan.

NASHVILLE, TENNESSEE

What's that smell? Who dropped a smelly bomb? Everything was going well until the third segment on the way to Heth AR when the odors started to be more noticeable. Caleb, screaming and laughing, said it was Uno. He has gas. With all eyes on Uno, he ran whimpering to the back of the RV while letting out a silent, smelly bomb. Honey, what did that dog eat? You took the dogs out this morning. I fed them the usual food, responded Ayo. Carmie, did you give the dogs scraps of your food again? Just a little, she said, turning while driving. Hey, keep your eyes on the road. We would like to get to the next stop in one piece. Babe, grab the air freshener and spray it to remove or at least mask that smell. Carmie began complaining. The RV feels like an oven! Are you sure the AC is working? Let's stop for some ice cream. The family was familiar with dry heat after living in the desert. The 92% humidity was something new and unusual to Carmie. Dad, when is the next stop? We are 16 miles from our next stop, which is in Forrest City, AR, at an RV stop so we can get serviced for the drive to Nashville, TN.

Carmie pulled the RV into the park and requested help from the attendant. Ayo wanted Carmie to learn to take ownership of the things she needed. She was going to need the skill of independence to survive in college. They went through similar steps to move the vehicle into the parking spot and get the required hoses connected. Carmie followed her Dad's example and gave the attendant a tip for helping. After a couple of hours' rest and some ice cream, they got back into the RV to begin the journey to Nashville. It was Ayo's turn to get them there safely. He had not driven for the day, so he was fresh and ready to drive his 3.33 miles to Nashville.

Ayo pulled into the RV camp outside of Nashville and requested support from one of the attendants to get the RV parked and hoses connected. Caleb smirked. By now, you should be a professional at parking the RV and connecting the hoses. There was no response; everyone was tired. It was the third day into the trip, and the energy was not the same as when they started. We are going to warm up some of the food we have in the cooler for dinner.

WASHINGTON, D.C.

Ashanti and Ayo were up at 6:00 AM getting breakfast ready. They both took the dogs for a walk, allowing them to do their business and run around for a while. The goal was to be on the road by 7:00 AM. The trip's final leg is 675 miles, estimated at 10:30 hours. The first segment is from Nashville, TN, to Morristown, TN, 225 miles for 3:18 hours. The second segment is from Morristown, TN, to Buchanan, VA, 225 miles for 3:28 hours. The third segment is from Buchanan, VA, to Washington, DC, 224 miles, for 3:42 hours.

I know you want to visit Kathy Smith on our way to Washington, D.C. Can we go to our new house first? I know it is a change from the original plan. We can then spend a whole week in Virginia, or she can spend as much time as needed visiting our new home. Can you share why we are changing plans, Ayo? It feels rushed, and we are tired from this road trip. Given Kathy's health challenges, it would be better to have quality time with her versus running in and out in one day. I think she would appreciate that. I will call Kathy and let her know of the change in plans. We can visit her in a week, or we can pick her up and drive her back to our home.

Ayo called out the driving order as the group prepared to head toward Washington, D.C. Ashanti will take the first segment, Caleb will take the second, Carmie will take the third, and I will take us into Washington, D.C. Let the journey begin.

GETTING SETTLED IN WASHINGTON, D.C.

The house looked exactly as in the photos reviewed by Ashanti and Ayo. The neighborhood was very diverse, and the tree-lined street was familiar. Ashanti and Ayo reflected on living in New York City when they were younger. Homes were closer than in Tucson. Do you remember hearing people flushing the toilets next door in NYC? Oh yeah, that was very interesting. The house in the Kalorama neighborhood was what they were looking for.

Ashanti reached out to her friend and coach, Melody. She shared that she lived in Barack and Michelle Obama's neighborhood. Melody said, Girl, you're on the come up. Melody is a female African American executive and organization coach who works primarily with African American executive women. She grew up in Northwestern Oregon in the United States with ancestral parents from the South. Ashanti shared that she is experiencing the feelings of impostor syndrome again and needs to get into a coaching session. She found that women of color often struggled with impostor syndrome because of the limited number of mentors and examples. Melody shared with Ashanti that her experience is not uncommon.

Girl, you have to be mindful of the tyranny of impostor syndrome. What do you need now? She asked. I don't know, replied Ashanti. What don't you know, responded Melody. First, I live in a neighborhood with celebrities and political stars. I am the new CEO of a company that is pioneering the latest technology. My children are growing up too fast, and I could be an empty nester soon. Ayo, he is on the short list for space exploration. My head is full of negative thoughts, and my brain-belly is erupting like a volcano. Where would you like to start, asked Melody. I want to start with living in a neighborhood of celebrities and political stars. Building community is important to me and my family, but I'm unsure how to approach these people. Do I call them "sir" and "ma'am" when I meet them? Perhaps there is a course to learn about the culture of the rich and famous. Hey Shanti, remember that we all have to take a poop. The sound of laughter could be heard over the video conference call. We tend to put people on pedestals when they're just like us, flesh and blood. I want to switch topics and talk about Kathy Smith. Do you remember Kathy, the former CEO of Avant-Garde Metaverse? Yes, I do. She is someone whom I should celebrate because of her mentorship, friendship, and love. Kathy Smith was the prior CEO of Avant-Garde Metaverse.

UNO, DUOS, AND DESTINY

Kalorama, Washington, D.C.

Alma had just finished sweeping the magnolia petals off the stoop when it happened.

The latch on their townhouse gate hadn't clicked shut the way it usually did. She had meant to check it but got distracted by a call from a client in Silver Spring—another urgent question about a property that wasn't even in escrow yet. She sighed, still balancing work and soul. But before she could bend down to gather the last handful of petals, the heavy thud of paws startled her.

Cielo santo—*Bruno!* Translated to goodness gracious, Bruno. The oversized Great Dane launched himself like a comet from inside the townhouse, galloping across the yard. In one miraculous leap, he cleared the wrought-iron fence that separated the Rivera home from the sidewalk. Alma dropped the broom. Across the street, a woman froze mid-step, holding two leashes with dogs on either end—a sharp-eared terrier mutt and a short, stocky pit mix, Uno and Duos, judging by the neon name tags clinking together. Both dogs perked up, tails wagging wildly, as the towering Great Dane barreled toward them in what looked like a majestic attack or perhaps a very enthusiastic welcome. Bruno, no! Alma yelled, chasing after him, apron flapping behind her like a cape.

Ashanti braced herself, knees bent, one hand clutching both leashes while the other reached into her coat—probably for a dog treat, or maybe a taser. Alma couldn't be sure. But before panic fully settled in, Bruno skidded to a halt a foot away from the trio. The big dog plopped down with a graceless *thud*, tongue out, tail thumping the pavement in rhythmic delight.

Uno barked once, Duos sniffed, and just like that, the canine summit commenced—full-body tail wags, playful hops, and a tangled mess of leashes and limbs. Oh my goodness, I am *so* sorry! Alma gasped, panting as she approached. He usually doesn't clear the fence. It's six feet! I swear, he's never done that before. Ashanti laughed in a melodic sound full of genuine amusement. It's okay! I thought he was gonna take me out like a linebacker. But look at them—instant besties. Alma chuckled, embarrassed but relieved. She tucked a curl behind her ear, steadying her breath. I'm Alma. Bruno's emotional support is human. She smiled, extending a hand. Ashanti. Uno and Duos' daily chaos coordinator.

They shook hands, their palms briefly pressed in the kind of warm contact that said *this could be something*. I haven't seen you before, Alma said. Are you new to the neighborhood? Ashanti nodded. I just moved in a few weeks ago from Tucson, Arizona, and recently purchased the brownstone on Bancroft. It's a lot. Welcome to the neighborhood, Alma said gleefully. I'm in real estate. But more importantly, she glanced down at the tangle of dogs. I make excellent *mofongo* and terrible cocktails, if you're ever in need of a neighbor who overfeeds. Ashanti's face lit up. That sounds perfect.

They stood there for a few beats longer, the dogs now a full-on knot of fur and tails. Alma saw something familiar in Ashanti's eyes. A flicker of stress, yes—but also resilience. The kind that came from starting over when you didn't want to. The type that Alma had felt the first time she sold a house and realized it wasn't just about square footage—it was about belonging. I'm starting something, Alma offered. A kind of mentorship circle for women, especially those new to D.C., or figuring things out after a significant change. I haven't fully built it yet, but I think it could be beautiful. Ashanti looked at her with a smile. Let me know when you do, she said. I guess I could use something beautiful right about now.

Bruno barked once, Uno barked twice, and Duos let out a loud sneeze like punctuation. The dogs had sealed the deal. Alma smiled. She'd come out to sweep petals and ended up planting a seed instead.

Later that evening, Ashanti curled into the corner of the living room sofa, legs tucked beneath her, a chamomile tea growing cold in her hands. Outside, the diplomatic streetlamps of Kalorama cast a soft, ceremonial glow on the brick-lined sidewalks. Inside, her new house still echoed with unfamiliar quiet. The brownstone hadn't yet learned her rhythms. Neither had she. Uno snored lightly, curled by the front door like a guard dog on break. Duos was belly-up on the hardwood floor, twitching through dreams, no doubt still chasing after Bruno, the Great Dane who had dropped into their morning like divine chaos. Ashanti tapped her phone awake and hit the call button. It rang twice before Ayo answered with that familiar tone of curiosity. Okay, Ayo said.

I need the full download. Something about a dog, a flying leap, and a woman with goddess energy? Ashanti laughed, the sound escaping before she could temper it. It was wild. I'm outside, walking the boys, minding my peaceful business—and out of nowhere, this enormous Great Dane clears a six-foot fence. Just —boring!—like it was nothing. Lands in front of me like, Hello, I am joy incarnate. I thought scooby doo right away. Oh wow, Ayo cackled. You nearly got tackled by a cartoon character. Was he friendly? Friendly? Ashanti glanced at Duos. He acted like we'd all been friends in a past life. Uno barked once, Duos went straight into play mode, and I stood there wondering if this was some new neighborhood hazing ritual.

And the woman? Ayo prompted. Alma. Alma Rivera. She comes rushing out after him, all flustered and radiant, wearing this flowy house apron like she stepped out of a vintage telenovela. Ashanti smiled at the memory. She was apologizing, breathless, but she had this energy about her. Like she'd seen the world and decided to love it anyway.
Ayo was quiet for a beat. So, you're smitten. Don't start, Ashanti warned, rolling her eyes with a smile. It wasn't like that. It wasn't a 'meet-cute.' It was a 'meet-kind.' Whew, Ayo said. Write that down. Ashanti stood and walked toward the kitchen, phone pressed between her ear and shoulder. She flicked the light off, the warm halo of the dining room now the only thing illuminating the space. She told me she's starting this mentorship circle, she said more quietly now. For women in transition. After a loss, life changes, stuff like that. I didn't even tell her about my mom and Kathy, but somehow, she got it.

Ayo hummed in that way she always did when something meaningful landed. That's divine timing, babe. That's not just someone passing you on the sidewalk. Right? Ashanti leaned on the counter, looking out through the back window into the darkness of the small garden. It felt like the beginning of something. Not because of the dogs or the neighborhood or the fact that she's precisely the kind of grounded presence I wish I had right now, but because it felt real, Ayo finished for her. Exactly. They let the moment breathe. I miss our place in the Old Pueblo, Ashanti said softly. This house feels foreign to me.

I don't even want to unpack. Maybe if I leave everything in boxes, I can pretend I'm just visiting. But you're not visiting, Shanti. You're becoming, Ayo said gently. We live here now, and it is home, our life. Maybe Alma? Maybe she's part of building what comes next. Ashanti exhaled, the kind of breath you didn't realize you were holding. She said I should stop by sometime. Try the terrible cocktails, stay for the mofongo. I think we should. Bring the dogs. Let them have their reunion tour. Ashanti smiled again, the first full one she'd had since arriving in D.C. You know, they didn't even growl at Bruno. Just wagged like they'd been waiting for him their whole lives. Smart boys, Ayo said. They know when something—or someone—is good.

THE GLOVE (AGUSTIN) AND THE CANDLE (ALMA)

The Southern magnolias along the quiet curve of Tracy Place were in full bloom. The white petals' fragrance filled the summer air. The Rivera home stood modestly among its stately neighbors—an ivy-laced brick townhome nestled between the stone grandeur of two embassies. Alma had always felt a little out of place in Kalorama. The neighborhood pulsed with polished affluence and guarded elegance, but their home hummed with a different rhythm—one made of *boleros*, prayer candles, and stories told over steaming cups of café con leche. From the kitchen window, Alma watched Agustin in the courtyard, crouched over the old cedar bench beneath the pergola. He was oiling his baseball glove again—his ritual, his anchor. The ivy curled over the brick wall behind him like it was listening.

Alma smiled. It was the 17th. You treat that glove better than you treat your knees, she called out in her familiar singsong as she stepped onto the terrace, wiping her hands on her apron. The air carried the aroma of *sancocho*, bubbling on the stove, mingling with the scent of damp earth and fresh jasmine. Agustin didn't look up. The glove never betrayed me. Alma didn't flinch. She knew his barbs were innocent and not aimed to wound. They were shields—his way of speaking truths he hadn't learned to say gently. She sat beside him on the bench, her hand brushing against his. You're allowed to miss it, you know. He set the glove in his lap and looked at her. In the dappled light, his eyes seemed darker, heavier. It's not the game I miss, he said. It's the clarity. When you're playing on that field, there's no second-guessing. No 'what now,' no 'what if.' Just you, the ball, and the moment. Alma reached for his hand, rough and calloused. You matter just as much here, *mi amor*. You always have. He didn't answer right away. In Kalorama, where senators walked their dogs and diplomatic cars glided past in silence, Agustin often felt like a relic, like someone misplaced in a neighborhood of clean lines and quiet ambition. But Alma? She had built a name here and sold homes to people who called her *magnetic*, *trustworthy*, and *brilliant*. And yet, even with her elegance, she'd never lost the softness of her Bayamón roots. She was the one who lit a candle for every client and cooked meals big enough for strangers.

I've been thinking about doing more, Alma said after a moment. Not just selling homes. Something bigger. Something for the girls who don't see themselves here. Agustin turned to her, surprised. You already do more. No, she said gently. I mean legacy. Teaching them that compassion and power don't cancel each other out. That they can lead with their soul. He studied her. Have you ever thought we're both trying to fix what we didn't have? She gave a soft laugh. Isn't that what everyone's doing?

Agustin looked out across the courtyard where the shadows grew long and soft. I've been dreaming about that academy again. A real place. For the boys. For the next me. I just— He hesitated. I don't want to start it too late. You're not too late, she said. You're right on time. The glove's still in your hand. He nodded slowly. It wasn't just a gesture—it was a letting go, a crack in the armor.

As Alma stood, she glanced over her shoulder toward the house. The window glowed gold with kitchen light. She reached over to the sill and lit the white candle kept there—her quiet tradition. A tiny flame flickered behind the glass, swaying like it, too, carried prayers in its light. Agustin rose, easing up with the stiffness of age but the posture of a man still fighting for a future. He placed the glove back into its display case with reverence and followed Alma inside.

In the heart of Kalorama—surrounded by power brokers and dignitaries—two souls plotted a future of their dreams. Not with wealth or politics, but with legacy. With healing. With dreams passed forward like torches.

KATHY SMITH NEWS

Strength is just softness that survived long enough to be useful. – **Kathy**

She didn't flinch. Not when the scan revealed what she already suspected. Not when the oncologist said the words *metastatic progression*. Not even when he gently added Stage Four. Kathy Smith, former CEO of Avant-Garde Metaverse, digital futurist, builder of worlds unseen and yet to be imagined, simply nodded and tucked her scarf more tightly around her neck. Let it begin, she whispered to herself, then she smiled.

Her reactions were not a denial or irony, just clarity. The kind she had cultivated over decades of leadership, mentorship, and change. The kind that came when time was no longer assumed, but reclaimed.

She waited until the evening to make the call. No press release. No dramatic social post. Just one short message to a close group, a circle of mentees and friends she had guided and loved over the years. Ashanti and Ayo were on that list.

Her voice on the message was calm, even warm: Hello, dear ones. I wanted you to hear it from me: my cancer has progressed. It's now metastatic—stage four. There's a treatment plan, but no illusions. I'm not interested in a fight. I've never seen life as something to conquer. Only to live—and live well. So I plan to do that. I'm going to take some time for the things I've postponed, the people I love, and the stories I still want to tell. No pity. Just presence. You are part of my light. I hope to be part of yours, for however long remains. Love, Kathy.

Ashanti read the message twice, standing by the large window in her Kalorama living room, her hands pressed tightly around a cup of tea she no longer tasted. She sounded at peace, Ayo said gently. She always does, Ashanti replied, tears pricking her eyes. " Even when she's walking into a storm. Ayo sat beside her. Then maybe it's not a storm to her. Perhaps it's just the next horizon.

Ashanti didn't answer. But in her chest, something swelled— not grief exactly, but a profound sense of witnessing. Kathy had always been more than a mentor. She was a blueprint. A compass. A living reminder that innovation without soul was empty —and that the strongest leaders were those who left doors open behind them.

Kathy's diagnosis did not stop her. If anything, it focused her. She spent mornings in stillness, practicing the meditation techniques she'd once taught her executive team during company retreats. Midday, she worked on her memoir, *Worlds Within Worlds*, a blend of personal history and reflections on building a metaverse rooted in empathy and ethics.

She began hosting small gatherings in her garden, wearing bright scarves and offering advice like sunlight, unasked for, but warmly received. She started sending letters to young women in tech she'd never met, offering encouragement, questions to wrestle with, and once, a quote scribbled on rose-pink station-ery: The point of vision is not to see forever, but to shape what you can see while you're still looking. And she did.

Even as the scans worsened, fatigue set in, her bones began to ache, and her appetite faded. Kathy Smith remained exactly who she had always been: present, potent, and unsparingly authentic.

Ashanti decided that she would visit Kathy the next day after receiving the news. I can pause work for a moment to visit my mentor and friend. The summer sun was setting, casting lavender hues over Kathy's townhouse. She brought a box of peppermint tea and a kente cloth throw.

Kathy sat wrapped in a fleece blanket, her skin pale but her eyes electric. You look like someone about to give a TED Talk, Ashanti joked, easing into the chair beside her. Only if they let me do it horizontally, Kathy quipped. Then silence, rich and unhurried. I don't want to say goodbye, Ashanti admitted, not like this. Kathy reached out, her hand light but deliberate. Then don't. Say thank you. See you in another form. Say, 'I'll keep the fire going. But don't say goodbye. That's not how legacy works.

Ashanti swallowed the lump in her throat. You were always one of the strongest women I knew. Kathy smiled faintly. Strength is just softness that survived long enough to be useful.

Kathy updated her living will. She transferred her shares to an educational trust. She asked that, when the time came, her funeral be streamed in virtual reality, *not because I'm afraid of death,* she said, *but because I've always believed in accessibility.* Kathy made sure her final public post read: *Stage Four. But not defeated. I built new realities from blank screens.* I think we can also create beauty from endings. Keep building.

THE LONG-
AWAITED VISIT

It had been five days since Kathy Smith arrived at the brownstone on Tracy Place. Ashanti insisted. You're not running anything for a week, she'd said, half-laughing, half-mothering as she wrapped Kathy in a hug that first evening. You're going to eat, sleep, and sit on our porch with your socks on inside out, and no one will say a thing. Kathy had only nodded, too tired to argue. That in itself had been a red flag.

And now, five days later, she found herself doing exactly that, sitting on Ashanti and Ayo's porch, in socks that didn't match, holding a cup of ginger tea that Ashanti made from scratch every morning.

Kathy called the first two days productive denial. Long, meandering conversations about AI ethics, the failures of tech bros, and the subtle genius of Toni Morrison's lesser-known essays. Ashanti had a way of anchoring their talks in the sacred ordinary—her laughter effortless, her insights sharp. It made Kathy feel human again. Ayo, always listening more than speaking, had been gently present. He'd join them after finishing his lectures at Howard, his backpack still slung over one shoulder, his mind already halfway into the metaphysical.

On the sixth morning, the weather changed. The sky wore the color of pewter, and the magnolia blossoms that had brightened the block earlier in the week now lay like fallen stars on the sidewalk. Inside the brownstone, Ashanti stirred oatmeal on the stove while Uno and Duos slept like sentinels beneath the windows.

You've been quiet today, Ashanti said gently. Kathy was perched at the table, chin resting in her palm. Just thinking, thinking, or carrying? Ayo asked, entering with his laptop in one hand and a steaming mug of chicory in the other.

I need to tell you both something, she said quietly. Ashanti stopped stirring. Ayo sat down, placing his mug gently on the table. Kathy looked up. Her eyes held no performance, only truth. I don't know how to navigate stage four breast cancer. The words hung in the kitchen like incense—heavy, sacred, unmistakable. She crossed the room slowly and sat beside Kathy, eyes already welling. Ayo didn't speak, but his eyes didn't leave Kathy's.

She continued, voice steady despite the tremor underneath. It's metastatic in my bones. The prognosis isn't immediate, but it's not long-term either. I've started treatment. I selected the most aggressive and experimental treatment. But it's real now. I didn't want to say it too soon because, for the first time in a long time, I just wanted to *be* and not explain. I want to be able to breathe. Ashanti reached over and took her hand. You don't have to inspire us, Kathy. Just let us hold space. Let us carry *you*.

Ayo leaned forward, resting his elbows on the table. You've spent your whole life creating worlds, Kathy. Now it's time to let people in. Especially when it's messy, that broke something in her, not in a shattering way but like a lock finally opening. I'm scared, she admitted, not of dying but of disappearing, leaving too many things unfinished—especially the *why* of everything I've built. You won't disappear, Ashanti whispered. You've already sewn yourself into this world and in us. In every young woman who's ever looked at you and thought, *maybe I belong here too.* Kathy exhaled. And in that exhale was the beginning of a new kind of healing. They sat there in silence, not as CEO and friends, but as kindred spirits, intertwined by time, trust, and now, truth.

Outside, the sky broke open, and rain began to fall softly against the windows. Ayo reached over and placed his hand on theirs. Then let's make the most of whatever time you have. If you're willing, maybe we can explore the 'why' together. With faith. With curiosity. With hope. Kathy didn't answer right away. She simply nodded, eyes glistening. Then, almost involuntarily, she whispered: Let it begin.

LEANING INTO THE FAITH, OUR PARENTS TAUGHT US

Ayo had come home from teaching classes at Howard University all day.

He'd taken the train, as he usually did on Thursdays, preferring the quiet hum of the Metro to the unpredictable frustration of D.C. traffic. The red line was half-full, commuters in varying stages of fatigue either scrolling through their phones or staring blankly out the windows. Ayo had pulled out his tablet to review a stack of student essays, carefully annotated in the margins— musings on science, sustainability, and one particularly ambitious freshman who tried to tie the laws of thermodynamics to ancestral trauma.

The train rocked gently as it pulled out of Gallery Place. Across the aisle, a boy in his teens sat hunched in a Howard hoodie two sizes too big, headphones in, nodding to a rhythm no one else could hear. Ayo wondered if the boy was heading to a night class or just wearing the brand like a dream still forming.

At Union Station, a woman in a long gray coat stood on the platform reading a worn Bible, lips moving in silent prayer. Ayo had paused as he stepped off the train, watching her for a beat longer than necessary. There was a quiet conviction in her, something that tugged at him. Something familiar. Not in the mind, but in the bones.

As he climbed the stairs out of the station, the city buzzed around him—horns, footsteps, the echo of a saxophone somewhere near Dupont Circle. But his mind kept drifting. First to Carmie, then to the words his father used to say, and then to that old notebook he hadn't touched in years.

By the time he reached the familiar curve of Tracy Place, Kalorama was settling into its hushed evening routine. Embassies glowed under vintage lamps. Cherry blossoms rustled gently in the breeze. At home waited a half-answered question. The house had grown quiet. Even Uno and Duos had settled into their twin nests of blankets by the fireplace, their snores low and rhythmic, like a heartbeat under the floorboards.

Ashanti stood at the window, one hand cradling her tea, the other resting on the sill, fingers idly tapping. Moonlight softened the room's hard edges. It was the kind of quiet that made you feel everything more deeply. The type that invited questions, you tried to ignore during the rush of the day. Behind her, Ayo sat on the edge of their bed, elbows on his knees, looking down at the floor like it had just told him a truth he couldn't unhear.

Ayo? she said gently, turning to face him. He looked up, startled from his reverie. Yeah. Yeah, I'm here. You've been somewhere else all evening. What's going on? He exhaled, long and low. Something's stirring in me, Shanti. I don't think I can keep ignoring it.
Ashanti crossed the room, curling beside him, their shoulders touching. I keep thinking about what happened with Carmie, he said quietly. How fast everything changed. How helpless I felt. Now we are in a new place. She is going to college with new people. He gave a big sigh.

The incident with Carmie certainly rocked our worlds and made me question my purpose for living in this world. We have achieved so much as a couple and individually that we have an abundance of everything we could ever dream of and then some. Babe, we need to lean into the faith our parents instilled in us. I know we have questions, and I certainly do not agree with everything said in churches. But something is missing, and my spirit man is prompting me to ask, seek, and know. Ayo, Ayo, Ayo, what's going on with Mister Scientific Mind? I never would have imagined that you would want a faith-based life. Carmie's experience haunts me, and I have to admit that I prayed that no harm would come to her or our family.

My father's pastor would preach that God was generous in giving us his commands to free us from death and protect us because of his great love for us. He would also say, "Put my thoughts under the governance of God's word, or my life will be governed by my thoughts."

I know, she said. It wrecked me, too. Ayo nodded. But it did more than just shake me. It made me have more questions about what all of this is for. Us. Our success. The things we've built. It's all beautiful, but it doesn't feel complete anymore. Ashanti tilted her head. What do you mean? I mean, he said, voice thickening, we have everything we ever dreamed of and then some: the house, careers, and this wonderful life. But something is missing. I'm missing something. I think—I know it has to do with faith. Ashanti blinked. You? Mister science, systems, and skepticism? He gave a small, sheepish laugh. Yeah. I've been having these dreams, Shanti. Not nightmares—more like callings. Echoes. Sometimes I hear my dad's pastor's voice, saying, "Put my thoughts under the governance of God's word, or my thoughts will govern my life." It won't let me go. She was quiet, letting the words sink into the air between them.

Ayo continued. He would say that God's commands weren't about control. They were acts of love and protection. I guess I'm finally starting to see that. I've been living so much by calculation that I forgot to ask why I'm even here. Ashanti reached for his hand. Bringing your dad's words into view is a lot. What brought this to the surface now?

Ayo hesitated. NASA called. They're shortlisting me for a space mission. Her eyes widened. What? It's still preliminary, but they're serious. If I say yes, it's a year-long commitment. Training, isolation, possibly orbit. I'd be gone. Far. Her grip tightened. Ayo, that's incredible and terrifying. I know. He paused. And if I go up there, looking down at all of this—I don't want to feel hollow. I don't want to just explore space while ignoring my soul. Ashanti searched his face. Ayo's emotions weren't just about space or success or even survival. What would it look like to be in a place of surrender? About anchoring himself in something that equations and oxygen levels couldn't calculate.

I've been praying, he admitted. Not out loud. Not like church. But real prayers. Raw ones. I even pulled out my dad's old notebook. He wrote down these Seven Principles for Kingdom Living. I never paid much attention to them before. But now? They hit differently. The prompts include questions like:
What will your spiritual legacy be?
Where will your loyalty lie?
What will be your priorities for your brief days on earth?
Do you want to meet Jesus knowing that you did just enough to get by?
Or do you want to meet Him knowing that you gave Him all you had, that you did everything you could to grow closer to Him, and to bring more people into His kingdom?

He leaned over to the nightstand, pulled out the weathered notebook, and handed it to her. Ashanti read aloud:
Principle One: Love God, people, and yourself. [Luke 10:27 NIV]
Principle Two: Be Holy. [1 Peter: 1:16].
Principle Three: Store up treasures in heaven. [Matthew 5:20 NIV]
Principle Four: Give generously. [2 Corinthians 9:7 NIV]
Principle Five: Live by the Spirit. [Galatian 6:22 NIV]

Principle Six: Let no debt remain outstanding except to love. [Romans 13:8 NIV]
Principle Seven: Leave an inheritance for your children's children. [Psalms 13:22 NIV]

She looked up at him, tears quietly welling. These are beautiful. They're weighty, Ayo said. And grounding. I want to live by them, not just know them. I want us to. Even if we still have doubts. Even if we don't have all the answers, Ashanti took his hand and placed it on her chest. Then let's do it together. Not out of fear. But out of love. For Carmie. For us. For whoever we're becoming. Ayo leaned forward, forehead pressed to hers. I don't know about making this, Shanti. Not of the mission. But what does it mean to surrender? She smiled gently. Surrender isn't weakness, babe. It's trust. And for the first time in months, something settled inside him—a peace, not loud or dramatic, but quiet and firm, like the ground beneath stars.

That night, while the city slept and the moon kept its watch over Kalorama, Ashanti and Ayo prayed together. Clumsy words. Long pauses. But real. It wasn't the start of religion. It was the return of faith.

WHAT WE BUILD
WITHIN

The rain fell gently outside the windows of Ashanti and Ayo's brownstone, a slow percussion on the glass. Kathy sat in the sunroom, wrapped in a soft quilt, a half-read devotional open on her lap. The book had been a quiet gift from Ashanti—a plain blue cover, no title, just worn pages and gentle, handwritten notes in the margins.

God's silence is not His absence, one line read. *Wait in the stillness. Wisdom dwells there.* She traced the words with her finger, then looked up to find Ayo entering with two mugs of tea. I made you the hibiscus one, he said, setting it beside her. Ashanti said it's your favorite. Kathy smiled faintly. She's right. She remembers the details.

Ayo pulled a chair beside her, leaning forward. You've been quiet this week. Thought I'd check in. Kathy closed the book. Calm is the only language I seem to speak lately. Sometimes quiet brings out truth, Ayo said. She looked out at the garden. I don't know what I believe, Ayo. My religious upbringing was Baptist, but attending church felt like a performance. And in tech? I learned that logic, results, and control are the currency. Now I'm here, watching my body fall apart, and I'm realizing how flimsy that currency is. Ayo nodded, listening.

I'm not trying to get 'saved,' she said, but I think I need to believe that something beyond me still holds value. That all this pain, this *process*, isn't just chaos. Ayo smiled gently. You're already on the journey. Faith isn't a straight line. It's a rhythm. Some days it's music. Other days it's static. Kathy leaned back and closed her eyes. You know what's strange? What you said reminds me of a moment, years ago. I've never talked about it. But I think, I think it's connected. Ayo folded his hands. Tell me!

In the quiet, I reflect on the Avant-Garde Realities, a startup that was then on the verge of folding. The Virtual Reality demo kept crashing, funding was drying up, and the CTO had just accepted a job offer from Google. A major investor in San Jose, CA, invited Kathy to meet to discuss potential funding. A tech conglomerate willing to buy their code outright and fold it into a defense simulation project. It was a golden parachute. But it meant surrendering her vision. It meant compromising. She stood alone that night, staring at the prototype headset, her thoughts spinning.

That was when Grace showed up. Grace Williams, her mentor from undergrad. A quietly powerful Black woman in engineering who also led Bible studies in the evenings. You didn't answer my call, Grace said, stepping into the garage with a bag of Thai food and a smile. Didn't know what to say, Kathy muttered. So you were gonna say nothing? Grace set the food down and pulled up a stool. Let me guess. Sellout offer? Kathy nodded. It could solve everything. Or it could destroy everything. Grace looked her dead in the eyes. Then you already know the answer. I don't think I believe in answers right now. That's fine, Grace said. Then believe in questions. Albert Einstein said, "If I had an hour to solve a problem... I would spend the first 55 minutes determining the proper questions to ask. Once I know the proper question, I can solve the problem in less than five minutes. Ask the ones that matter. Don't ask, will this save me? Instead, focus on, will this *make* me?

Kathy exhaled, her shoulders finally dropping. That night, she didn't sleep. But by sunrise, she had made her decision. She would build it her wa**y**. Vision intact. Integrity intact. Even if it meant bootstrapping from scratch again, she would not let fear be her architect. Kathy opened her eyes. I turned down a buyout that could've made me a millionaire at twenty-nine, she said. Everyone thought I was crazy. But I couldn't live with building something rooted in fear.

Ayo smiled. You trusted a deeper voice. I think, Kathy said slowly, I'm ready to hear that voice again. Not the one in my head. The one inside my heart. The one that says: *I've got you.* Ayo reached into his satchel and pulled out a small card. A folded page with seven handwritten lines. He handed it to her.

The Seven Principles for Kingdom Living

1. Love God, people, and yourself.

2. Be Holy.

3. Store up treasures in heaven.

4. Give generously.

5. Live by the Spirit of God.

6. Let no debt remain except love.

7. Leave an inheritance for your children's chil-

dren.

Kathy stared at the page. Start anywhere, Ayo said. But don't go alone. She didn't cry. But something in her cracked beautifully. Like ice thawing on a spring day. She looked at Ayo. Thank you, she whispered. For showing me that surrender isn't weakness. It's going over to the winning side. Can I keep these? Indeed, Ayo said. Outside, the rain stopped. Sunlight broke quietly across the windowsill, warm, unassuming, but full of promise.

WEAVING THE FUTURE – UWAZI'S GLOBAL RISE IN IMMERSIVE LEARNING

In the heart of the Old Pueblo, amid the warmth of adobe walls and the spirited pulse of innovation, Uwazi emerged— not merely as a startup but as a clarion call for equitable, immersive learning. Co-founded and later led by the visionary Ashanti Mwendo, Uwazi's innovation started to dismantle barriers to education and skill development using the transformative powers of AI, VR, AR, and XR technologies. At a time when conventional methods of education struggled to reach the marginalized, Uwazi promised an audacious future: immersive, inclusive, and inspiring.

From its early days, Uwazi's mandate was clear: education must not be a privilege dictated by geography, economy, or infrastructure. By marrying empathy-driven design with cutting-edge technology, Uwazi aimed to create a platform where learning was not only accessible but deeply engaging and transformative.

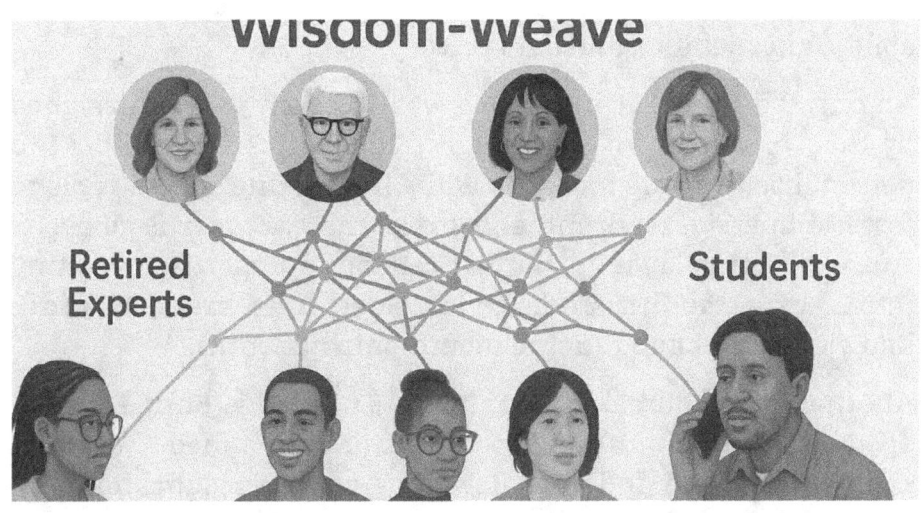

THE UWAZI HACKATHON: FORGING PURPOSE THROUGH INNOVATION

The Accessible Education and Skill Development hackathon became the crucible where Uwazi's ideals took tangible form. A convergence of minds—design thinkers, coders, educators, and community representatives—crafted solutions that addressed real-world issues. It was not simply a contest but a movement. Teams from diverse backgrounds developed solutions that embodied the hackathon's guiding principles: inclusivity, sustainability, affordability, and data privacy.

Among the standout initiatives was Wisdom-Weave, designed by the Threads of Wisdom team. This platform utilized AI to personalize learning journeys while integrating VR/AR tools to foster immersive environments for learners across the globe. Its true innovation lay in its human-centric approach—connecting retired experts with students in underserved areas to bridge knowledge gaps and nurture mentorship networks.

Another groundbreaking solution, Knowledge-Bridge, developed by a team of multidisciplinary students, aimed to connect skilled artisans in underprivileged regions with global markets. Through immersive storytelling and digital showcases, the platform highlighted not only the craft but also the culture and humanity behind each creation, weaving education and entrepreneurship into a single, compelling narrative.

Perhaps the most heartfelt innovation was Harmonic Code, envisioned by twins Carmel and Caleb, both on the Autism Spectrum. Blending Leet speak and musical symbols, their solution offered children with ASD a novel way to express themselves, transforming communication into an art form of sound and symbol. Harmonic Code resonated with educators, therapists, and families globally, opening doors previously locked by the limitations of traditional language.

GLOBAL TRACTION AND REAL-WORLD IMPACT

What began as a localized event in Tucson's vibrant community quickly spiraled into a global movement. Uwazi's platforms attracted the attention of governments, non-profits, and corporate learning departments around the world. From rural classrooms in Sub-Saharan Africa to digital training centers in Southeast Asia, and corporate offices in Scandinavia to indigenous learning initiatives in South America, Uwazi's immersive tools were being embraced and embedded.

Global traction wasn't accidental—it was intentional. Uwazi's leaders strategically formed partnerships with NGOs and public institutions, creating implementations that tested and validated their platforms across diverse socio-economic contexts. Corporations used the tools for leadership training, onboarding, and cross-cultural coaching. Government agencies incorporated them into re-skilling initiatives for unemployed youth and veterans transitioning to civilian life. These weren't pilot programs —they were living ecosystems of learning.

Uwazi's growth journey was not without corporate intrigue. Initially incubated under Avant-Garde Metaverse (AGM), Uwazi flourished under Ashanti's leadership and the technological stewardship of CTO Clive Schmid. A cybersecurity investigation and internal political shifts eventually led to Uwazi's independence—an evolution marked by both growing pains and profound liberation.

Post-independence, Uwazi's growth accelerated. Its Gross Value Added (GVA) surged, with the company becoming a staple in conversations about the future of learning in the Metaverse. Ashanti's elevation from interim to permanent CEO reflected the board's confidence in her ability to guide Uwazi through uncharted territories, both technologically and ethically.

Harmonic Code

HARMONIC CODE: A SYMPHONY OF INCLUSION

Harmonic Code became the flagship that encapsulated Uwazi's ethos. Therapy centers adopted the new technology, including inclusive classrooms and homes globally. Children who once struggled to be heard were now singing their thoughts—literally and figuratively—through a medium that honored their uniqueness. Carmel and Caleb's story traveled from hackathon anonymity to global recognition, though questions of intellectual property and ethical stewardship simmered behind the scenes. Nevertheless, their innovation underscored the potential of immersive technologies to transform not just how we learn but how we connect and communicate.

UWAZI'S LEADERSHIP CULTURE AND FORWARD PATH

What powered Uwazi's ascent was not just innovation, but intentional culture. Leaders like Zen Chan, Chief Engagement Officer, ensured that community voices remained central to product evolution. Data scientists like Marisela Rivera-Guzman ensured that machine learning understood learners without bias. And the vigilant eye of cybersecurity expert Adrian Turner safeguarded the digital sanctity of user experiences.

Their collective vision envisioned a world where education was decentralized, personalized, and experiential—a world where a child in Nairobi could receive the same quality coaching as a teenager in Tokyo. A world where indigenous ancestral stories could be preserved through immersive history lessons and arti-sanship passed down through virtual mentorship.

Knowledge-Bridge
linking artisans to global markets

LEGACY AND THE ROAD AHEAD

As Uwazi expands its global footprint, it remains anchored in its founding principles. The seeds sown in the Old Pueblo continue to sprout across continents, each bloom a testament to what is possible when technology serves humanity. The journey ahead includes partnerships with HBCUs, expanded multilingual content, and the development of biometric feedback systems for adaptive learning. Yet, its most vital mission remains unchanged: to democratize access to education and skill development, not as a luxury, but as a right. In the echo of digital classrooms and the harmony of melodic messages, the spirit of Uwazi endures—a symphony of stories, a tapestry of transformation, and a venture that dares to dream the world into a more just, immersive, and intelligent future.

THE SUMMER BEFORE EVERYTHING

The air in Kalorama was thick with the fragrance of magnolias during the summer months—lush canopies of old trees casting long shadows over stone sidewalks, and townhouses humming with life behind bright hydrangeas and crepe myrtles. It was a quiet neighborhood, tucked just enough away from the fast pace of the Capitol to feel like its own slow heartbeat.

For Carmel MWendo-Joseph, or "Carmie" as her family often called her in these tender in-between moments, it was a summer of standing at the edge of everything—adulthood, academia, ambition. She had just turned sixteen. In weeks, she would officially begin her first full year at college. But for now, she was simply a teenager navigating time with her family, soaking up the city's rhythm and history like breath before a long dive.

From mid-June to mid-August, their season of exploration began. With her twin brother, Caleb, and often guided by Ashanti or Ayo, Carmel moved through D.C.'s museum circuit as if it were an ancient city of knowledge waiting to be deciphered.

The Smithsonian National Museum of African American History and Culture

They began there. Carmel stood transfixed before Emmett Till's casket, her fingertips curled tightly into her palms. Caleb was quiet beside her, an unusual silence. They both took slow steps through the history galleries, each section deepening their understanding of both inheritance and resistance. I thought I knew, Carmel said softly. It's not just history, it's weighty and pulsating. Later, they stared at a wall of Black icons—musicians, politicians, poets—and Carmel's eyes lingered on Vice President Kamala Harris. One day," she said to Caleb. He nodded. I believe you.

National Air and Space Museum

Ayo beamed here, guiding them through hangars and launching capsules with the enthusiasm of a boy on the moon. They saw the Apollo 11 Command Module, then stood beneath the model of the Mars rover. Finally, Carmel paused at the exhibit on women in space. Mae Jemison wasn't the last, she whispered. She was the first of us. They took turns using astronaut glove simulations. Caleb dropped a wrench. Carmel tightened a bolt. It was silly, but meaningful. She could feel the dream shaping inside her—technology, exploration, and a voice that reached further than gravity allowed.

Hirshhorn Museum and Sculpture Garden

Carmel had expected to be bored here. Instead, she was overwhelmed. One room featured looping videos of voices, and digital art installations that pulsed with sound and identity. One piece, an AI-generated visual map of family trees across the diaspora, brought her to tears. I can feel the code humming with stories, she told Caleb. He nodded, drawing his sketchpad from his bag to scribble his impressions. The experience became a new rhythm between them, Carmel with her thoughts, Caleb with his drawings, side by side but on their journeys.

PREPARATION AND REFLECTION

By August, Carmel was preparing for school. Her list was precise, her schedule color-coded, her vision board trimmed in pink and green for Alpha Kappa Alpha goals. Yet one afternoon, while sipping lemon-ginger tea on the porch with Ashanti, she let out a long sigh. I'm nervous. Ashanti lowered her book. Good! What if I'm too young? What if I'm just a kid trying to wear a grown woman's shoes? Ashanti chuckled. You're not wearing anyone's shoes, Carmie. You're making your path. That takes courage, not age. Then Ayo came out with a box of photos—Ashanti at a protest in New York, him in graduate school, pictures of them young and driven and unsure, too. Carmel traced her fingers along the glossy edge of her family's story and felt herself exhale. She wasn't alone, but built from dreams that stretched backward and forward.

Before school began, they returned once more to the Museum of Natural History, primarily for Caleb's sake. But in the Fossil Hall, as they stood before a massive woolly mammoth, Carmel smiled. Even extinction leaves an echo, she said. That's what I want to be, an echo of something good, even long after I'm gone. Caleb grinned. You're not extinct yet. You're just starting. And so, with journals filled, memories packed, and a quiet confidence blossoming in her chest, Carmel prepared to step into her next chapter, not just as a student, but as a storyteller, a builder, a bold and brilliant force in the making.

CARMIE - LETTER TO MYSELF

August 17 – Kalorama, D.C.

Dear Charismatic Carmel,

Tonight is quiet.

The kind of quiet that feels like the world is holding its breath, waiting for your next step. You are ready to go through the door, your notebooks stacked, your hair freshly braided, and your playlist is already titled *Commute Vibes Vol. 1.* The moment you've dreamed about is here. College. For real. But before you start, take this moment. Take it slow. It will go by faster than you can imagine. Well, that's what my parents say.

This summer, you grew in ways no schedule could capture. You didn't just visit museums—you walked through them like archives of your own story. You stood in rooms soaked with struggle and triumph, and you didn't just look—you felt. The weight of history. The brilliance of Black creativity. The sound of possibility in your ears is like a heartbeat.

You learned things you didn't expect. That grief can live inside joy, reminding you that you are, in fact, not too young. That silence is sometimes strength, not absence. That museums are less about artifacts, and more about echoes.

You saw Kamala Harris's portrait and whispered, One day. You touched the edge of a space shuttle and thought, Why not me? You wept after watching the memorial video for Emmett Till.

Now I ask, am I able to carry the work forward?

Caleb and I shared the city as if it were our map of wonder, he with his mobile device, I with my curious voice. We didn't always agree, and that's okay. We're twins, not twinsies. But he saw me. He always sees me. Hold that close. And mom? She may not always say it the way you want to hear it. But her caution is just love with a shield. Her dreams for you are genuine. Stitched into the way she watches your face when you speak. Trust that. Dad sees the stars in you because he knows what it means to reach for them.

So here's what you'll need when classes start and the summer of change is behind you and everything suddenly feels too different:

> Remember your summer in Kalorama.
>
> Remember who you were before they asked you to prove it.
>
> Remember that your softness is not a weakness—it's calibration.
>
> Remember that I don't know yet is a complete sentence.
>
> And remember: *You belong.*

This letter isn't advice. It's a mirror. A pause. A whisper from this version of you to the one that's about to bloom like the magnolias. You're not becoming. You're unfolding. So go ahead. Be brilliant. Be bored. Be bold. Be still when you need to be. Be exactly who you are with no apology and no permission requests. And if you ever feel lost, reread this.

Love you already, Charismatic Carmel

TREASURES NOT MADE OF GOLD

It was a warm, breezy Sunday in D.C. The kind that made the streets around Howard hum with life: jazz floating from open windows, lineups at the local brunch spots, and students lounging in the grass with books open but barely read. Caleb Mendo-Joseph had expected to spend the morning sketching in the park, earbuds in, world off. But that changed with a casual invitation from his friend Jalen, a sophomore from Brooklyn with a relaxed energy and a heart for people. Hey, Jalen said over breakfast at a local cafe. Have you been to The Table? It's a non-denominational church a few blocks off Georgia Ave. Diverse. Real talk. Good music. I think you'd dig it.

Caleb hesitated. Church had always felt complicated. Abstract. But Jalen had never steered him wrong. I'll go, Caleb said. But only if they don't try to hand me a tambourine. Fair, Jalen laughed. But you might catch yourself singing anyway. The Table was nothing like what Caleb expected. There were no stained-glass windows, no robes or pulpits. Just folding chairs, warm lighting, voices from every culture, and a praise band that fused gospel, Afrobeat, and lo-fi jazz. The pastor, a woman in her forties with box braids and bright sneakers, stepped up and smiled like she already knew everyone by name. She opened her message with a quiet reading from Matthew 6:20:

> But store up for yourselves treasures in heaven, where moth and rust do not destroy, and where thieves do not break in and steal.

The message unfolded like a gentle provocation. The pastor spoke of legacy, of doing work that outlives applause. She asked the congregation: Are you spending your days stacking clout and comfort, or are you building the kind of love, service, and justice that even time can't erode? Caleb listened, brow furrowed, the verse circling in his mind like a riddle.

What does that mean exactly? Caleb asked Jalen as they strolled back toward campus. What are the treasures? Why would you need treasures in heaven? Where would they be stored? Jalen thought for a long moment. I used to think it was just about, like, doing good stuff so you could go to heaven after you die, he said. But now? I think it's about the kind of *impact* you leave. Things like kindness, honesty, and helping people when no one is watching. Those aren't tweets. They're deposits in a kind of eternal bank account. Caleb raised an eyebrow. So spiritual Venmo? Jalen laughed. Sure. Except you can't see the balance, but you *can* feel it growing.

Later that night, Caleb brought it up at dinner. The pastor said Moth and rust destroy the wrong kinds of treasures. So what does it mean to have treasures in heaven? Perhaps values or purpose, as Ayo looked over at Caleb. Ayo leaned forward. It's a wisdom tradition. In Yoruba spirituality, we also speak of living in a way that keeps your Orí, your higher self, aligned with your destiny. It's not that different. Ashanti tilted her head and smiled. Isn't that one of your dad's seven principles, Ayo? Yes, it is, he replied. Ayo chuckled. The concept the pastor was teaching is to live in a way that honors something bigger than ego. Bigger than today.

Caleb sat back, the puzzle slowly taking shape. So, treasures aren't what we stack. They're what we plant. Ashanti nodded. Exactly! Some trees won't bear fruit until long after we're gone. But they still matter. That night, Caleb opened his tablet and began to draw. He sketched a treasure chest, but instead of gold, it held a collage of intangible things: a hand reaching to lift another. An elder's eyes. A worn library card. A spiral galaxy. A small sapling growing from a cracked sidewalk. At the center, a glowing heart. He titled the piece: Treasures That Moths Can't Touch.

COMMUTING
TO CAMPUS

Each morning, as the sky yawned open over Kalorama, Ayo stood at the wrought-iron gate of their brownstone, backpack slung over one shoulder and coffee in hand. Beside him, Carmie clutched her satchel and water bottle, earbuds dangling, curls pulled into a high puff. Come on, Daddy, she grinned. "If we miss the red line again, I'm blaming you and your slow sips.

Ayo laughed, locking the gate behind them. I'm building up my thoughts for the day. Research doesn't power itself. They took the short walk to the Metro station in rhythm—father and daughter, two dark-skinned reflections of each other, descending the stairs into the pulse of Washington, D.C. The train platform buzzed with its usual mosaic of commuters: government staffers in polished suits, students in sweatshirts, immigrants speaking Urdu, Amharic, and Spanish—the morning symphony.

Okay, your turn, Ayo said, stepping onto the train as the doors opened. What'd you learn yesterday? Carmie rolled her eyes playfully. You think I'm gonna let you turn the red line into a quiz room? I've got tenure," Ayo teased. Which means I can ask ungraded questions. She grinned. Alright. I learned that Dr. Njeri, in the global studies department, studied in Ghana for three years and has a Fulbright Fellowship. She's gonna introduce me to her niece, who's studying virtual fashion. Ayo's eyebrows rose. Virtual fashion? Now that's a new one. It's the future, Daddy—clothes you wear in the metaverse. I thought I barely understood Gen Z. Turns out Gen Z doesn't even understand Gen Z. They both laughed.

Carmie gazed out the train window. You know what's wild? Every time we get closer to campus, I see more people who look like me. It's comforting. Like, the world makes a little more sense. Ayo nodded slowly. That feeling of mirrored excellence, of shared skin and shared brilliance, was precisely why he had chosen Howard University. It wasn't just history. It was the present. It was a possibility—poured into brown faces, polished into genius.

He had joined Howard to lead cutting-edge STEM research in ethical AI and data equity. But he stayed for the culture. For the *impact*. His partnership with Uwazi, a Pan-African tech research institute, was starting to gain momentum. They planned to expand tech literacy in underfunded D.C. schools and create youth innovation labs across Wards 7 and 8. But Ayo's vision wasn't just for the city. It was for his family.

For Caleb. Think your brother would survive a morning like this? Ayo asked casually. Carmie snorted. He wouldn't pass the turnstile. They both laughed again, but Ayo's heart sank a little. Caleb, his sixteen-year-old son, had become a tangle of contradictions—brilliant but guarded, passionate but withdrawn. Every invitation Ayo made—to visit the campus, sit in on a lecture, tour the labs—had been met with a mumbled *nah* or a flat-out *not my vibe.*

But lately, something had shifted. Caleb had started asking questions. Nothing direct—just fragments. Carmie, what's that café you always go to? Is it true that Howard has a student who started a sneaker company? Carmie never pressed. She just answered, shared her stories, and let him listen. Then, one Tuesday morning, without warning, Caleb appeared at the front door —hoodie half-zipped, earbuds in, slouched backpack and all. I'm coming with y'all, he said, not looking up. Carmie's eyes widened. For real? Ayo suppressed a smile. Let's go!

The train ride was quiet, Caleb nodding along to his playlist while pretending not to be curious. But Ayo caught him glancing at the murals in Shaw, the mosaic of people on board, the conversations happening across languages and generations. When they stepped onto Howard's campus, Caleb paused, frozen, even. Black and brown students filled the quad. Some with braids. Some with backpacks covered in anime patches. A girl laughed into her phone in Nigerian Pidgin. A boy skated past wearing a STEM is Black History shirt. Caleb stared. And for the first time in a long while, Ayo saw awe behind his son's usually guarded expression. Didn't know it'd feel like this, Caleb muttered. Like what? Carmie asked. Like, I could fit here.

They started walking toward the science building. That's when it happened. A student exiting the Engineering Lab paused and did a double-take. Yo, that's an Akai MPC Live in your hoodie pouch? Caleb blinked. Yeah. You know it? I use the same model. I'm in Dr. Green's wearable tech course—we're doing sensor integration for live sound tracking. Caleb's jaw dropped. Wait, you're building *sound-reactive gear*? The student grinned. Wanna see the lab? Caleb looked to Ayo, then Carmie, like he needed permission but didn't want to ask. Ayo raised an eyebrow. Go. Explore.

That night, back home, Ayo sat on the porch, sipping his tea. Carmie stepped outside, hoodie wrapped around her. He's watching Howard YouTube videos, she whispered with a smirk. Ayo looked up, blinking in surprise. Seriously? Carmie nodded. And he followed that student on IG. He mentioned wanting to start prototyping his 'sound skin' idea. Whatever that means. Ayo leaned back in the chair, the city night buzzing faintly around them. Three train tickets. One shared story. And maybe, just maybe, a door opening.

FREQUENCIES OF THE FUTURE

The lab smelled like solder and ambition. Caleb sat hunched over a workbench in Howard's Innovation and Design Lab, his hoodie sleeves pushed up, exposing a tangle of wires and a prototype glove embedded with motion sensors. Across from him, Jalen—now his campus guide, mentor, and playlist rival—adjusted the settings on a software dashboard.

Okay, rerun it, Jalen said. Caleb flexed his fingers and waved his hand in a slow arc. The LED lights embedded in the palm flared in response, pulsing in rhythm with the ambient track playing on the studio speakers. Jalen grinned. Yo. That's it. You've got reactive frequency syncing. Caleb's eyes lit up. Imagine this at live shows. Like, wearable beats. The music moves with you. Exactly, Jalen said. Your sound-skin concept? That's next-gen performance tech. You could patent this. Caleb looked up, stunned. For real? Jalen nodded for real.

Caleb leaned back in his chair, heart thudding—not just from the tech, but from the possibility. This place—these people—were seeing him. Not just as a rebel kid with a music obsession, but as a creator. A visionary. It felt like being heard for the first time in a language he didn't know he spoke.

Meanwhile, just across campus, Ayo stood before a room full of community leaders, faculty members, and Uwazi Foundation delegates in a roundtable hosted in the School of Engineering's Global Partnerships Wing. As the sunlight filtered through the historic windows, a sense of anticipation filled the room. Among the distinguished guests were community leaders from Washington, D.C.'s Wards 7 and 8, advocates, educators, and civic organizers whose dedication to equity and empowerment had long shaped the city's narrative. Their presence underscored the importance of the moment: Dr. Ayo Joseph was preparing to deliver a keynote presentation focused on the needs of local communities. For these leaders, Ayo's journey was not just inspirational—it was personal, a reflection of the brilliance rising from the very neighborhoods they served.

He clicked to the next slide in his deck: Digital Bridges, Cultural Roots: STEM Access in Southeast D.C. Howard's partnership with Uwazi, Ayo began, isn't about charity. It's about alignment. It's about taking the genius we already have in our communities —the ones who code beats in bedrooms, who fix phones from scratch, who build hustle into everything they touch—and giving them tools to scale that genius. Heads nodded. The Howard University partner with Uwazi, Dr. Kwesi Adebayo, tapped notes into his tablet, eyes glimmering. Zen Chan, Uwazi's chief engagement officer, nodded in agreement.

Ayo continued. Through this initiative, we'll launch two youth innovation hubs by fall, one in Ward 7, one in Ward 8. These won't be after-school programs. They'll be ideal studios. Places where students can prototype, research, remix, and launch. Professor Njeri from Global Studies raised a hand. How do we include cultural literacy into tech development? We can't separate innovation from identity. Ayo smiled. Exactly. That's why we're building the curriculum with local artists, faith leaders, and elders. We're not just teaching code—we're teaching *context*. From African fractals to West Indian sound systems, from Anacostia storytelling to AI ethics, this program will center culture *as* curriculum. Applause broke out, not out of formality, but recognition of the new possibility in the community. For Ayo, this was more than a project. It was a full-circle moment. Howard wasn't just where he worked. It was becoming the epicenter of how his family, his research, and his faith intersected in a tangible mission.

That evening, Ayo stepped into the brownstone just as Carmie and Ashanti were setting the dinner table. The scent of turmeric and roasted garlic lingered in the air. Where's Caleb? Ayo asked. Upstairs, Ashanti said with a knowing smile. He hasn't stopped talking about the lab. Carmie leaned in. He said he wants to create a short film with reactive music wearables. I think he's gonna pitch it to Dr. Kwesi Adebayo and Dr. Njeri from Global Studies. Ayo paused, absorbing the quiet miracle of it. His son—once indifferent, detached—was dreaming in blueprints and BPMs.

He headed upstairs and found Caleb in his room, earbuds in, nodding to a beat as waveforms danced across his laptop screen. A prototype glove lay on the desk beside a crumpled sketchbook filled with circuitry diagrams and song lyrics.

Ayo knocked lightly. Caleb pulled out one earbud. Yo. Are you good? Caleb smirked. Yeah. Jalen said if I clean up my code, we can pitch the project next month. Ayo stepped inside, crossing his arms. Are you thinking about applying? To Howard? A beat passed. Caleb shrugged. Maybe. I dunno. It's different there. Feels like home without all the rules. I still have to feel it out. Ayo chuckled. Sounds like a yes-in-progress. Caleb smiled but didn't answer. Instead, he put his earbuds back in and returned to his screen. The music thumped softly. As Ayo turned to leave, he caught sight of a quote written on a sticky note above Caleb's monitor: The future belongs to those who hear it before building it. Below it, in Caleb's handwriting, were the words: Heard it. Building it.

THE RHYTHM OF US

The glove never betrayed me. –**Agustin**

Latin music poured through the open French doors, its rhythm infectious and joyful. A blend of merengue and salsa spun from the speakers as laughter bubbled from the patio, where family and friends mingled beneath strings of warm café lights. In the lush backyard of the Rivera home, everything seemed to exhale —time slowed, hearts softened, and memories kneaded into the air like bread rising. Bruno, the Great Dane, galloped in figure eights across the yard, barking playfully at Uno and Duos, who chased each other around the lemon trees like synchronized chaos. Near the grill, Agustin manned the tongs like a maestro, flipping pork shoulder and chorizo with a practiced hand while Alma shouted at him from the kitchen, ¡No dejes que se seque, Gus! - Don't let it dry out!

Inside, Ashanti and Ayo leaned against the kitchen island, eyes gleaming at the vibrant chaos around them. Alma handed Ashanti a steaming bowl. Mofongo, she said with pride. Crushed plantains, garlic, pork cracklings—mashed together in love and served in a pilón, the wooden mortar. You eat it hot, with a bit of broth, and never with regrets. Ashanti dipped a spoon into the golden mash and let out an audible hum of satisfaction. The tastes have flavors of history. It is, Alma smiled. It's my grandmother's recipe. She said it could cure anything from heartbreak to back pain. Across the kitchen, Ayo raised a glass filled with something tropical and effervescent. What *is* this? he asked Agustin, who had just walked in, sweat glistening on his brow and a proud gleam in his eye.

Agustin clinked his glass to Ayo's. Ron con frutas. White rum, mango nectar, a little guava, lime, and just enough sugar to remind you life is sweet. Also known as 'Run with fruits.' Dangerously smooth, Ayo said. Like my merengue, Agustin grinned.

Outside, Caleb and Carmel were seated at the patio table, both half-scrolling and half-snapping pictures of their parents, who were now fumbling through a merengue routine Alma was leading. Wait. Wait—Mom is trying to do a turn, Carmel said, zooming in with her camera. She's gonna crash into Dad, Caleb muttered, eyes locked on the unfolding hilarity. Sure enough, Ayo tripped over his foot and bumped into Ashanti. Both burst into laughter, almost collapsing as Alma clapped enthusiastically. They are *so* not ready for the island, Caleb added, amused. Send me that video, Carmie said, already posting it to her story with the caption: *#MerengueMadness #ParentsUnplugged.*

Later, after the music slowed and the stars hung lower over the yard, the four parents sat around the fire pit, sharing drinks and softer stories. So, Alma asked, twirling the straw in her nearly empty glass, How are you two doing? Potential space travel, Kathy's health news, and all the headlines about your company's growth. Ashanti glanced at Ayo, then back at Alma. Grateful. Excited. Tired, but glad we met you. Ayo nodded. Kathy's health news hit us harder than we expected. She shared a kind of wisdom we didn't know we were borrowing from until now, the possibility of it being gone. Agustin rested his drink on his knee. I lost my coach to that terrible disease. He wasn't famous. But he taught me the game and how to walk away from it with dignity.

You were a ballplayer?" Caleb chimed in, finally looking up from his phone. Agustin's eyes lit up. Once. Shortstop. Played for a few years in the minors. I even got called up for a short run in the majors. No way, Caleb said, suddenly animated. Wait, what era? Early '90s. Yankees system. El Paso, Tampa, and a couple of weeks with the big team. Caleb stared, impressed. That's unbelievable! Do you still have your stats?

Agustin laughed. My son made me a baseball card for my 60th birthday. I'm sure it's wildly exaggerated. I'd love to see it sometime, Caleb said. I'm deep into analytics. My music coding overlaps with statistical modeling—kind of like sabermetrics meets sampling. Agustin raised his brows. You're speaking my love language now. Ashanti leaned toward Alma. That's the first time I've seen Caleb light up about baseball since he was six. Agustin has that effect, Alma whispered. He doesn't talk much, but when he does, it's pure gold. The four parents toasted their glasses, the crackle of the fire joining the soft background hum of an old Héctor Lavoe, a Puerto Rican salsa singer, recording now playing inside. Alma looked around and smiled.

This rhythm, she said, is the rhythm we forget to keep. The joy between milestones. The people who remind us we're more than our missions. Ashanti squeezed her hand. To keep rhythm. To protect each other, Alma replied. And above them, stars blinked in rhythm, like distant lanterns, celebrating quietly in time.

BALANCING ACT

Leadership is not the absence of resistance. It is the art of remembering who you are in the face of it. –**Ashanti**

Ashanti stood barefoot in the kitchen at 5:47 a.m., one hand stirring the steel-cut oats on the stove, the other thumbing through a Slack message on her phone. A global operations update had just dropped in her inbox—something about a supply chain bottleneck in São Paulo. Her mind ticked through options even as the aroma of cinnamon and cardamom filled the air.

From upstairs came the faint sound of Caleb's music—always a beat early, like him. Down the hall, Carmie's bedroom light clicked on, and a soft gospel tune floated through the vents. In twenty minutes, the house would hum with layered conversations, misplaced notebooks, forgotten passwords, and the rhythm of a family preparing to greet the world.

But this was her moment—the in-between. Ashanti exhaled

deeply.

By 8:00 a.m., she would be Ashanti MWendo, CEO of *Uwazi*—
an international company connecting African diaspora communities with regenerative development projects. She would speak
on panels, negotiate policy proposals, and mentor three younger
executives—all while being expected to look effortless in heels
and high-stakes diplomacy.

But here, in her brownstone, she was just mom and wife. Sometimes, a woman is balancing on a tightrope of expectation and
quiet unraveling.

At 7:15 a.m., Ayo entered the kitchen, freshly shaven, glasses
slipping down his nose, tie draped over his shoulder like an
afterthought. Coffee's hot, Ashanti said without looking up. I
was hoping you'd say that. He kissed her cheek and poured a
mug, watching her out of the corner of his eye. You've got that
look again," he said gently. What look?

The one that says, I'm solving five global problems before breakfast and still wondering if I packed Carmie's lunch. She smirked,
pushing her hair behind her ear. Only five? I must be slipping.
Ayo leaned against the counter. Have you ever thought about
stepping back? Just for a little while? She turned to him. Have
you ever thought about the moon turning off its light? He nodded, amused but not dismissive. Fair enough. But even the moon
wanes sometimes. Ashanti softened. I don't want to disappear,
Ayo. I just want to be enough for them and us. He took her hand
and squeezed. You already are. But let's not pretend this is easy. It
wasn't.

That evening, after meetings, panels, and a quick pivot to resolve
an executive conflict in Ghana via WhatsApp, Ashanti returned
home exhausted but full. She kicked off her heels by the door and
found Carmie at the kitchen table. She climbed the stairs and
peeked into Caleb's room. He was on a call with Jalen, excitedly
talking about integrating tactile feedback into his music wear-

able glove. Ayo was already home, stretched across the couch with a stack of student submissions he was grading.

Later, after dinner and laughter and spilled juice and one minor sibling argument, Ashanti slipped into their bedroom and closed the door behind her. She and Ayo lay in bed, the lamp casting a warm glow as the night settled over them. You know, she said, her voice quiet, I used to think balance meant making everything equal. Giving 100% at work and 100% at home. But now I believe balance is knowing when to give 20% in one place so you can provide 80% in another—and trusting the people you love to meet you where you are. Ayo turned to her, eyes soft. That sounds like surrender. Maybe, she said. But not in defeat. In *trust*. He kissed her forehead. Then let's keep trusting. Outside, the city murmured. Inside, they held each other—public figures in the world, private anchors at home. Two people are still learning how to hold space for greatness and gentleness at once. The balancing act continued. But tonight, it didn't feel like a performance. It felt like a partnership.

INNOVATIONS
AND SETBACKS

The top-floor conference room of the Uwazi International Center for Innovation shimmered with early morning light. Floor-to-ceiling windows cast shadows across the table where leaders from five countries sat poised with tablets, journals, and nervous energy. Ashanti stood at the head, her palms pressed together as she took in the moment. It was more than just a quarterly summit. The unveiling of Uwazi's boldest initiative yet.

Welcome, everyone, Ashanti began, her voice calm but commanding. Today, we launch Project Sauti. The word Sauti, meaning voice in Swahili, appeared on the screen behind her, followed by its mission: Tech-powered civic platforms for African diaspora youth to co-create local solutions. The idea had been months in the making. Under Ashanti's leadership, Uwazi had shifted from a passive funding body to an active design partner, working with communities in Accra, Baltimore, Nairobi, and Port-au-Prince to create a living ecosystem of innovation hubs. Each node reflected the culture, needs, and vision of its people— a concept built on decentralization, ethics, and community.

The vision is no longer just about access to tools, she continued. It's about building agency. It's about training designers of systems, not just users. And we do it through storytelling, technology, and local governance. Applause broke out. Some clapped slowly, skeptically. Ashanti caught it. She always did. She moved to the next slide: A solar-powered mobile studio in Ghana. A biometric-free identity wallet pilot in D.C., and a community blockchain marketplace in Kenya that utilizes oral history validation. The oral history validation was an experiment using the process of assessing the accuracy, reliability, and credibility of information obtained through oral history interviews. The air buzzed with cautious hope.

But by week's end, the glow began to dim. First came the headlines: *Tech Philanthropy or Digital Colonialism? Critics Question Uwazi's Expansion Model.* Then came an anonymous leak, internal feedback from a Nairobi-based coordinator frustrated that Western consultants overwrote the local team's design. The post went viral on activist channels within 24 hours. Ashanti read the report alone in her office, jaw tight. Then came the board meeting. We support your vision, Ashanti said Selam Toure, a respected elder and the longest-serving board member. But transparency must be part of our innovation. Are we scaling too fast? A junior board member from Paris added. Are we getting pressure from competitors? The competitors' media campaign is painting them as the more 'grounded' alternative in diaspora development. Ashanti remained composed, but her silence was heavy. After the meeting, she retreated to the rooftop garden at the family's home. Ayo met her there, knowing her patterns. I hate this part, she said. The distortion. The cheap narratives. As if we're just dressing imperialism in Afro-futurism. Ayo placed a hand on her shoulder. Then counter the story. Not with sound-bites. With clarity. With your voice.

The next morning, Ashanti called for a private internal review, without the PR team and brand consultants. Just community partners, youth fellows, and field directors. They gathered in a hybrid town hall, live in D.C., streaming from Accra, Johannesburg, and Kingston. Ashanti stood without notes. We've built something bold, she said. Bold doesn't mean perfect. We made choices that didn't reflect our values, and I take full responsibility. But let me be clear, Uwazi is no gatekeeper to innovation. It is a vessel. Vessels must repair themselves when they crack, not hide. She paused. So from this day forward, every design team must be co-led by a youth liaison from the target region. Every initiative will include a cultural historian, not just a data scientist. We will publish our internal critiques, not to shame, but to model what growth looks like. Chat threads lit up with affirmations. Field partners nodded. Some cried. Ashanti knew, in that fragile space of exposure, that she had led with principle and not with perfection.

Later that evening, she updated the project's status report herself. At the end of the document, she typed that leadership is not the absence of resistance. It is the art of remembering who you are in the face of it. Then she closed her laptop and joined her family for dinner, her sanctuary. Carmie recounted a student senate debate. Caleb talked about integrating West African drum patterns into his sound skin prototype. Ayo passed the sweet potatoes and made a dad joke that got no laughs and two eye rolls. Ashanti smiled. She was still balancing, refining, and building something no algorithm could quantify.

REEVALUATION

Legacy isn't about being famous. It's about making someone braver because you showed them a way forward. – **Caleb**

Caleb's fingers danced over the console in his small studio workspace, tucked into the back room of the family's brownstone. Wires snaked across the desk like vines, and a prototype of his *SoundSkin 3.0* glove blinked to life. With every subtle movement of his fingers, the LED fabric shimmered and pulsed in time with the beat looping through his headset—an unreleased track he'd been building with Jalen and an Afro-house artist from Nairobi he met through Uwazi's network.

Success has come quietly over the last six months. An independent tech-art showcase featured Caleb's first wearable beat demo —a short write-up followed in a youth innovation blog. And last month, he received a small grant to develop an open-source version of his glove tech for public schools. The win felt surreal.

But with each step forward came a knot of uncertainty. Last week, a panel judge at a virtual pitch competition praised his concept, then asked a simple question: Are you in a degree program? No, Caleb had replied. The pause that followed stung more than he expected. Although the panelist moved on, the tone lingered, suggesting that credibility still lived in classrooms, not bedrooms-turned-labs. He'd told himself college wasn't for him. He still believed that. But sometimes, when Carmie came home glowing from a debate, or when their parents shared stories from their educational journeys, he wondered: Was he enough without the credential? The question returned often. But he never let it stall him for long.

This morning, he had a workshop scheduled at the Uwazi youth hub, teaching teens how to build emotion-reactive audio samples using only a tablet and a sensor bracelet. It wasn't a lecture. It was a creation. That was how he taught: by doing. He strapped on the glove, took a deep breath, and reminded himself: This is a classroom, too, and I am the learning facilitator.

Pretty. Powerful. Possible.

The soft rustle of magnolia leaves whispered outside her bedroom window as Carmel, barely sixteen, clicked *Submit* on her final exam of the semester. A moment passed. Then came the notification she had been waiting for: Final Grades: 4.0 GPA Her fingers hovered over the keyboard, her breath caught between pride and disbelief. She had done it—a perfect first semester at Howard University, a historic feat for a student her age. But tonight, that was only part of the celebration. Pinned to her vision board, printed in emerald and pink, was her genuine aspiration: Alpha Kappa Alpha Sorority, Incorporated - *Service to all humanity.*

It wasn't just about sisterhood. It was a legacy. It was Kamala Harris. It was Toni Morrison. It was the elegance of Michelle Obama's nods of respect. It was the late Sheila Jackson Lee, a longtime Democratic congresswoman from Texas and an outspoken advocate for Black Americans. It was the way the AKAs carried themselves across time, like a current of grace wrapped in intellect, poise, and purpose. And Carmel knew—she was ready to follow in their footsteps.

The thought had taken root during a student-led event on campus. Carmel, standing in the back in her crisp blazer, watched the Alpha Chapter of AKA perform a tribute to trailblazers in American history. The sound of their voices harmonizing, the controlled pride in their step routines, the palpable command of space—it stirred something deep inside her. One of the seniors, an AKA with the kind of quiet command that made rooms pause, caught Carmel watching. She smiled and said simply: You belong here. Carmel went home that evening floating. She knew who she was. But now, she also knew who she was becoming.

The kitchen in the Kalorama house was warm with the scent of cinnamon tea and roasted cashews. Carmel sat at the breakfast bar, eyes glowing. Ashanti was reviewing a document on her tablet, her reading glasses perched delicately at the edge of her nose. Mom, Carmel began softly, her voice carefully controlled. I've decided I want to pursue membership in Alpha Kappa Alpha.

Ashanti looked up slowly. Carmel, you're sixteen. I know. But I'm a full-time student. I've proven myself. I meet the academic requirements. I have community connections and I'm ready. Ashanti took a breath and lowered the tablet. You're brilliant. That's never been in question. But pledging a sorority, even one as honorable as Alpha Kappa Alpha, requires a level of emotional maturity that most adults spend years building.

Carmel's shoulders tensed. I am mature. You and Dad made sure of that. You don't trust me? It's not about trust, Ashanti said, her voice more tender now. It's about timing. That world, it's rigorous and political. A sisterhood, yes, but also filled with scrutiny. You're still growing into yourself. I don't want you shaped by pressure before you've had space to bloom naturally. But that's the thing, Carmel pushed back. AKA wouldn't shrink me. It would stretch me. It's not about parties or popularity. It's about purpose. It's about aligning myself with women who have *done the work*, who embody the legacy I want to walk in. Ashanti's silence was long. You're my baby, she whispered. The world doesn't always handle gifted Black girls gently. I want to give you more time.

That evening, as the sky turned amber over the city, Ayo joined Carmel on the back porch. She sat curled under a quilt, earbuds in, staring into the fading light. He sat beside her, wordless at first. Then: Your mom means well. You know that, right? I do, Carmel said. But it's like she wants to keep me in the greenhouse forever. I'm trying to reach sunlight.

Ayo smiled faintly. You are the sunlight. He turned to face her more fully. Carmel, I remember when I told my father I wanted to study in New York City. He said no. I went anyway. It changed my life. Not because New York City made me, but because I chose it. Carmel turned to look at him. Should I do it? You should continue to carry yourself like the woman you want to be. If AKA aligns with your spirit, then pursue it with your whole heart. Not to prove anyone wrong, but to affirm who you already are. Pretty, powerful, and possible, Carmel said quietly. Ayo raised an eyebrow. That sounds like a platform.

Later that night, Ashanti stood outside Carmel's room, listening to her daughter on a video call with her mentor from the honors program. She heard the ease in her tone, the intellectual spark in her voice, the discipline in her questions. She was, unmistakably, growing up. Ashanti pressed a hand to her chest and whispered: Maybe you're more ready than I want to admit. She knocked softly. Carmel opened the door, uncertain. Ashanti stepped inside and placed something on her desk. It was a small journal notebook with an ancient crest on the cover. Use this to write your why, Ashanti said. Every reason you want to join. Every fear. Every strength. Don't just chase the legacy. Define it. Then I'll know you're ready. And so will you. Carmel smiled, tears rising. Thank you, Mom. Ashanti kissed her forehead. Whatever letters you carry, remember—your name already carries a legacy.

CARMEL WHY STATEMENT

I was eight when I first saw Vice President Kamala Harris on a debate stage. I remember my mom pausing the TV and saying, That's Alpha Kappa Alpha. She's walking in the footsteps of a powerful sisterhood. At the time, I didn't fully understand the depth of what that meant, but I remember how my body straightened up, like something ancient had whispered to me through the screen.

Now I'm sixteen. I am a full-time college student. A creator. A daughter. A twin. A girl growing into the fullness of her womanhood—and the woman I see ahead of me is someone who carries grace without apology, service without ego, and strength without noise. She is, in many ways, the embodiment of what I see when I envision Alpha Kappa Alpha Sorority, Incorporated.

My desire to pursue membership is rooted in alignment with the organization's values. Alignment with women who have shaped culture, policy, education, and community, not just for themselves, but for generations. I want to be part of a lineage that values legacy as much as it does sisterhood. I don't just want to admire it from the outside—I want to contribute to it. I wish to pledge not for status, but for stewardship, because I believe in the responsibility that comes with excellence.

As a co-creator of Harmonic Code, I've seen firsthand how a seed of an idea can become a bridge for once voiceless children. And I know that kind of impact grows in gardens where sisterhood cultivates trust, where iron sharpens iron, and where young Black women learn to rise without needing to step on anyone to get there.

Some people say I'm too young. And maybe in some ways, I still am. But I've also spent my life surrounded by excellence. My mother breaks barriers and expectations daily. In my father, whose curiosity defies gravity. And in myself, every time I choose discipline, dignity, and boldness in rooms where I am the youngest, but never the smallest.

I want to join Alpha Kappa Alpha because I know I'm ready to be a vessel of service, leadership, and legacy. I want to link arms with women who transform vision into action. Who moves the needle on what's possible?

I want mentorship. I want to mentor. I want to grow. I want to shine with my sisters, not alone.

In the words of our Vice President: I eat 'no' for breakfast. In my mother's words: Whatever letters you wear, your name already carries legacy. Today, I decided to walk with both. With all that I am, and all that I'm becoming,

– Carmel MWendo-Joseph

PREPARATIONS FOR SPACE TRAVEL

Ayo, reread the email three times before standing. It was December, and winter began to settle in.

NASA-HBCU Space Education Initiative — Final Candidate Confirmation.
Subject: *Welcome to the Horizon Vanguard Cohort, Professor Joseph.*

The message was simple. Understated, even. But the implications unraveled like stardust in his chest. He was selected. Ayo, short for Ayokunle (eye-OH-koon-lay) Joseph, a Howard professor, father of two, eternal pragmatist, was going to space. Not for tourism but as an educator. A bridge between Earth and the next frontier of learning.

The mission, officially called Horizon Vanguard, would send a small, international crew aboard the experimental Athena IX spacecraft—NASA's newest low-orbit research vessel equipped with modular, AI-augmented lab pods. Ayo's specific task? Evaluate the efficacy of STEM instruction in altered environmental conditions, consisting of low gravity, reduced oxygen, and variable light cycles. How would young minds absorb data? Could we prepare future students not just to imagine other worlds but to thrive in them?

Two weeks later, Ayo stood in a press conference auditorium at Howard University, blinking under stage lights as the university president delivered the news. Today, we mark history. Professor Ayo Joseph, esteemed faculty of Applied STEM Education, will become the first Howard scholar selected for space research under the NASA-HBCU initiative. His journey is not just personal, it's collective. He takes our students, our ancestors, and our vision with him.

The crowd of students erupted into cheers. Carmie, seated front row, wiped a tear before beaming with pride. Caleb, standing in the back with his arms folded, offered a subtle nod, the kind he reserved for things that truly impressed him. Ashanti MWendo, ever the composed diplomat, smiled proudly but felt her stomach coil inward. As the world celebrated, she was calculating oxygen levels, re-entry speeds, and her husband's departure from Earth.

I BELONG HERE – PRETTY IN PINK, GORGEOUS IN GREEN

The envelope was thin. Slim enough to slip beneath the stack of college flyers and summer leadership mailers. But Carmel knew; she felt what it carried. Her hands trembled just slightly as she ran her thumb under the edge of the envelope flap, heart tapping out its rhythm. One glance. That was all it took. Then the scream came, unfiltered, unchoreographed, *pure*. I belong here!

Carmel's voice echoed through the upstairs hallway like sunlight cracking through stained glass. Her room—usually a quiet cocoon of notebooks and lo-fi playlists—had become a sanctuary of shouted joy. Mom! MOM! I belong here! Ashanti bolted up the stairs, thinking something had broken, possibly Carmie herself. Carmie?! Baby, what! But Carmel was already flying toward her, envelope flapping, cheeks wet with hot, holy tears. She threw her arms around her mother's waist and held her like a girl holding onto history. I got in, she whispered through laughter and sobs. I got in. Alpha Kappa Alpha. Mom. I belong.

Ashanti froze for a heartbeat, and then the weight of Carmel's words settled deep in her chest like an anthem passed from mother to daughter. She pulled her baby girl closer. Oh, my sweet Carmel," she whispered. "You were born for this. Ashanti wasn't an AKA herself, but she'd walked alongside sorors, mentored by women whose grace and strength were rivaled only by their service. She knew what pink and green meant: dignity, legacy, sisterhood, and power rooted in purpose.

She cupped Carmel's face and asked gently: What's next for you, Carmie? Carmel stepped back and opened the letter again, re-reading the words like scripture: In the letter, it says I must acknowledge and accept the invitation. Then the Graduate Advisor will guide me through the Membership Experience process. I'll receive the schedule, what to expect, and how to prepare. She beamed. It's all outlined—authorized activities, intake steps, everything official and sacred. Are you ready for this chapter in your life? Ashanti asked. Carmel nodded. Then shook her head. Then nodded again—faster this time. I can't wait! she said, jumping up and down. I can't wait!

The noise drew Ayo upstairs. He poked his head into the room, brow lifted. What's going on up here? I belong, Dad! Carmel shouted. I received my acceptance letter for Alpha Kappa Alpha Sorority, Incorporated! Ayo's face lit up like a sunrise. He walked over and gathered her into a hug that wrapped around generations. Your grandmother would be doing backflips in heaven right now, he said. Carmel grinned. Backflips? Really? Well, spiritual backflips. They laughed, all three of them, Ashanti wiping her eyes, Ayo clapping rhythmically, and Carmel dancing in place like she couldn't stand still under the weight of her joy.

Later that night, Carmel sat at her desk, a candle burning beside her, and opened her journal. She titled the page: Pretty in Pink. Gorgeous in Green. She wrote: Today, I joined a river. A river of women who carved paths through concrete. Who held picket signs in one hand and degrees in the other. Who mentored girls like me before I even knew what the word "sisterhood" meant? I'm not pledging to be perfect but to be present, and to serve. To lead. To rise. This isn't about colors. This is about calling.

In the weeks that followed, Carmel read everything she could find about Alpha Kappa Alpha's founding, its illustrious 20 pearls, the Alpha Chapter at Howard University, and the community impact of service-led programs like HBCU for Life and #CAP. She printed quotes from Ethel Hedgemon Lyle and taped them to her mirror. She listened to old sorority step performances with wide eyes and bobbing shoulders, wondering what her line name might be. Every time she walked past a woman in pink and green on campus, she held her breath a little. Not out of intimidation, but recognition.

Ashanti and Ayo watched their daughter grow louder in her confidence and quieter in her doubt. Carmel began to glow in ways that had nothing to do with outfits or GPA. She had always been brilliant. But now, she was becoming rooted. You walk differently now, Ayo said one evening, handing her a cup of warm tea. Do I? Carmel asked, sipping. You walk like you know who's walking beside you—even when no one's in sight.

The Membership Experience would begin in the spring. Carmel was ready—folders organized, journal blank pages waiting, heart open. As she folded her letter and placed it inside a keepsake box, she whispered again to herself: I belong here. Somewhere between the halls of Howard and the ancestral halls of legacy, twenty pearls gleamed just a little brighter.

UWAZI YOUTH INNOVATION HUB

The Uwazi Youth Innovation Hub in Ward 7 buzzed with after-school energy. The space was a former library, renovated with exposed brick, modular workstations, muraled walls, and a glass-paneled studio called *The Resonance Room* where young creators experimented with music-reactive technology and storytelling. Kathy stood near the entrance, watching a group of high schoolers clustered around a smartboard as one of the interns demonstrated a prototype of an AI language assistant designed for multilingual neighborhoods. The room smelled faintly of cinnamon pastries and 3D printer resin. Impressive, right? Ayo stepped beside her. More than that, Kathy whispered. It feels necessary. The room felt charged with something more than innovation; you could sense possibility. It was not the curated, expensive kind from a Silicon Valley product demo. But real, grounded possibility, rooted in Black brilliance, community storytelling, ancestral wisdom, and raw hunger for change.

As they moved deeper into the space, Kathy passed two young girls painting circuitry patterns on canvas in the Maker Lounge, a teenage boy livestreaming a beatmaking session, and a group of middle schoolers in VR headsets exploring ancient Ethiopian architecture in an immersive cultural history experience. Each of those kids, Ayo said, was told they weren't STEM material. Not anymore. Now they're inventing what's next.

Kathy was quiet for a long time. Finally, she said, this is what I wanted Avant-Garde to become—a platform for expanding reality, but emotionally and spiritually. Ayo turned to her. You opened the door for a new generation, realized through Uwazi. She met his gaze. Ayo smiled, this inspiration has left something that breathes life into generations.

That night, back at the brownstone, Kathy sat at Ashanti's writing desk, pen in hand, and notebook open. No keyboard, no intelligent assistant. Just ink and breath and memory. She began to write.

To the one who will stand where I once stood:

Names fade, but legacies ripple. I hope you feel at home in the rooms you build, the code you write, the student you mentor, or the risk you take when no one else sees your vision. I used to believe success was scaling upward. The goal was always the next innovation, the next funding round, the following release number. But life taught me something different. What matters is what lives when you stop building.

So I'm passing this to you. Dream like your ancestors prayed for you. Lead like healing is a strategy. Teach like your wisdom was always meant to be shared. If you ever wonder whether you're enough, know this: I've seen the future in the eyes of children who had every reason to give up. Still, they created. Still, they imagined. Still, they believed.

So must you.

With love,
Kathy Smith
Avant-Garde Metaverse, Former CEO
Uwazi Fellow, Builder of Worlds, Seeker of Spirit

She folded the letter and placed it inside a clean envelope, sealing it with wax. On the front, she wrote: For the Future.

Ashanti walked in moments later with two cups of hot cocoa, pausing when she saw the letter. Kathy smiled and held it up. Just in case I don't get to say it in person. Ashanti set the mugs down and wrapped her arms around her. Then let's make sure we do. In the silence that followed, two women, one recovering, one preparing to release, sat together at the intersection of courage, clarity, and the sacred power of *legacy*.

LIGHT, LOVE, AND LIFT-OFF – A KALORAMA HOLIDAY

In the historic, tree-lined streets of Kalorama, where century-old townhomes stood like dignified storytellers of D.C.'s past, the MWendo household glowed with warmth and vibrant music. Twinkling lights wrapped around the wrought iron balcony, the scent of cardamom and plantains drifted from the kitchen, and the laughter of children echoed down the cobbled sidewalk.

It was Christmas Eve, but it was more than that. It was a celebration of Christmas and Kwanzaa, a joyful punctuation to the end of the school term for Carmel, and a deeply meaningful send-off for Ayo, selected for astronaut training. In just a few weeks, he would leave Earth, figuratively now, and soon, for the rigorous journey that would culminate in his seat aboard the Athena IX.

But tonight the house is full of people, cultures, memories, and one quiet current of bittersweet love. The first to arrive were Alma, Augustin, and Bruno, whose entrance was as rhythmic as expected. Augustin carried a small speaker that immediately began pulsing with *parranda* music. Alma wore a crimson shawl embroidered with gold stars, and Bruno, full of mischievous holiday energy, darted straight for Uno and Duos, the family's corgis. ¡Mis mejores amigos! Augustin shouted. Uno yipped. Duos rolled belly-up.

In the kitchen, Ashanti and Melody stirred pots side-by-side.

Ashanti wore a kente apron over a soft green jumpsuit; Melody had tied her locs up with a gold ribbon and moved with the precision of both chef and coach. Are you sure you're feeding people or preparing for launch? Melody joked, nodding at the spread. Both, Ashanti said with a smile. He'll need memories of flavor up there. Then came Kathy Smith. She was thinner now. Her stride was more careful. But her eyes, always sharp, scanned the house with a glow of recognition and affection. Ayo greeted her with a long, steady embrace. Ashanti's hands didn't let go for a moment longer. You made it, Ashanti whispered. I had to, Kathy replied. I want to see what the future looks like when lit by love.

The Christmas tree sparkled in one corner of the sitting room, decked with ornaments from every chapter of their lives: musical notes from Harmonic Code, an astronaut helmet with Ayo's name etched in tiny silver thread, carved wooden angels from Ghana, and a ceramic star with HOPE painted in seven-year-old handwriting from Carmel. Beside it, a Kinara was placed prominently on the mantle. Ashanti had explained it earlier to the kids and guests unfamiliar with Kwanzaa. Tonight, they would light the candle for Umoja—Unity.

Because no matter where we're from or what we're facing, she said, we are stronger together. In joy and sorrow. In legacy and lift-off. Ayo led the candle-lighting. One by one, they called what they wanted to unify. Family and future, said Carmel, holding her friend Amara's hand. My body and my courage, whispered Kathy, who then smiled softly. Earth and stars, said Ayo, voice sure and grounded.

Later, as plates passed and music shifted from soul to salsa, Ayo slipped away to check on Kathy. She was in the study, wrapped in a blanket, the firelight reflecting in her eyes. Are you doing okay? He asked gently. I'm at peace, she said. I've seen so many seasons. And this—this—this is my favorite. Watching you soar, Ashanti shine, and the children thrive. It's everything. You gave us this foundation, Ayo replied. We're just building on the grace you taught us. Kathy squeezed his hand. Build it boldly, Kathy whispered.

As the night waned, Alma gathered everyone into the living room. Agustin has prepared a performance, she announced. Agustin stepped up in a red bowtie and held a homemade maraca. Behind him, Caleb tapped a beat on a djembe, Carmel sang a riff from her Harmonic Code app, and Bruno began a joyful rap in both Spanish and English:

Feliz Navidad, let the candles glow, Unity and joy, let the rhythm flow! Uno and Duos bark and spin. Bruno stood and looked curiously.

But love is the rocket we're launching in! The room erupted in laughter and applause.

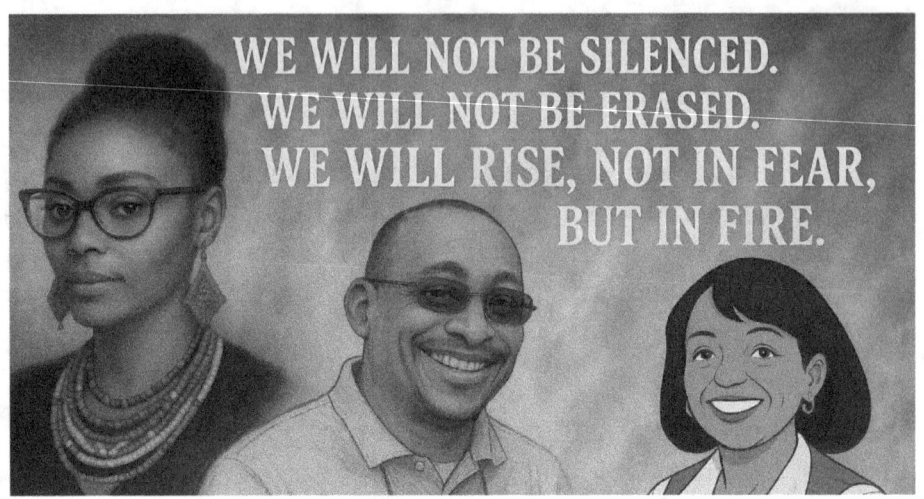

WE WILL NOT BE SILENCED.
WE WILL NOT BE ERASED.
WE WILL RISE, NOT IN FEAR,
BUT IN FIRE.

ASHANTI'S BLESSING

Before the night ended, Ashanti stood with Melody beside her and raised her glass of bissap. To those we love and those we miss. To Kathy, our anchor and angel. To Ayo, our explorer. To the children who remind us why we dream. And to every light, every lesson, and every legacy. May this house remain a place of joy and refuge. And may the stars welcome our stories. Ase! Someone called. Amen, came another. And Ad Astra, Ayo added with a wink.

The house in Kalorama, nestled beneath the winter stars, sang with stories—past, present, and yet to come. It was a place where Christmas glowed and Kwanzaa grounded, where cancer didn't steal joy and space was no longer the final frontier, but the next classroom. And in that house, on that night, light did not flicker; it danced.

TRAINING BEGAN
IN A FEW WEEKS

At the Space Academy for Educators housed in the North Campus Residence Hall at the University of Alabama in Huntsville (UAH), Ayo entered an elite cohort of nine scientists, engineers, and one poet from Kenya who would study neuroplasticity in microgravity. They called themselves the Edgewalkers. The training was going to begin with six months of intense training. The educator astronaut program usually takes about two years of evaluation. However, since the educators were not going to function as full astronauts, an abridged training period was deemed acceptable. Eventually, the cohort would transfer to the Astronaut Training Facility at NASA's Johnson Space Center.

Each day began at 4:30 a.m.

- Cold immersion. High-altitude acclimation chambers.
- Aerobic circuits in weighted suits.
- Surgical-like precision drills in zero-g simulators.
- Neuro-response tests under emotional stress.

The hardest part wasn't physical—it was psychological. Isolation pods. Sensory deprivation exercises. Even dream recording trials—mapping cognitive response to altered REM cycles. After one particularly grueling module, he confessed to his trainer, "This feels more like soul boot camp than space prep. That's precisely what it is, the trainer replied, space strips you. What's left has to be enough.

Back home, dinner had changed. Carmie hovered, offering him

herbal teas and research on cardiovascular recovery. Caleb watched him more closely now, as if trying to memorize his walk. Ashanti wanted to play it cool, but Ayo noticed the new books on the coffee table: Trauma, Grief, and the Unknown. The Physics of Re-Entry. Letters to an Astronaut's Family.

One night, after the kids had gone to bed, she broke. I'm scared, Ayo, she whispered. I've watched you stretch across countries, missions, and institutions. But this? You're going to leave gravity behind. What if he reached for her hand? I know. I'm scared, too. But every part of me believes this is the right thing, not for legacy but for the next generation of learners. Ashanti nodded slowly. Then let's build the tether now. So wherever you are, we're still connected.

ATHENA IX SPACECRAFT

Athena IX was a marvel—modular chambers, constructed with nano-reinforced memory alloys, adjusted to the astronaut's vital readings in real-time. The ship ran on a hybrid of solar and ion propulsion, allowing for longer orbital durations.

Its gravity engine—still in testing—could simulate Earth-like pull in short bursts. Ayo's lab, located at the heart of the *Athena IX* Learning Pod, features biometric chairs, haptic feedback tables, AI tutors, and augmented projection interfaces.

His module bore a nameplate: Uwazi Initiative - Classroom Alpha.

It gave him chills. Two days before his final departure for launch preparation, Ayo gathered the family in the living room. No phones. No distractions. He looked at Carmie. Keep asking questions that no one has answers to. That's how progress begins. He turned to Caleb. Keep building. Even when the world doesn't understand the blueprint yet. Then to Ashanti. And you, you are the ground beneath all my orbit. When I float, it's your love that brings me home. They held each other for a long time.

As he stepped into the transport bound for the Kennedy Space Center, crowds of students from Howard lined the gates, waving banners and playing drums. Caleb uploaded a new sound sample to Ayo's watch, ambient tones built from their family's heartbeat recordings. Carmie slipped a note into his duffel bag: Bring back something we can't see, but can believe in. Ashanti stood tall, hand on her heart. Ayo Joseph, scientist, father, educator. He closed his eyes, preparing to rise above Earth not for glory, but for understanding. Not to escape home, but to extend it.

BEYOND THE HORIZON: AYO'S ASCENT AND THE UWAZI CLASSROOM IN ORBIT

It began with a nameplate. Fixed just beneath the reinforced viewing port of a sleek, titanium module aboard the Athena IX, it read: Uwazi Initiative - Classroom Alpha.

Ayo Joseph stood before it in his pressurized flight suit, heart pounding—not from fear, but from the awe of stepping into a reality long written in the pages of speculative fiction. His classroom, his lab, his sanctuary of learning and curiosity, now orbited 200 miles above Earth aboard a marvel of science and human cooperation. And it all began with a dream that education could and should reach for the stars, literally.

It was a declaration of purpose. A symbol that learning had left the cradle of Earth and now orbited among the stars. For Dr. Ayo Joseph, that nameplate was not only a milestone in his professional life, but it was a mission to test how immersive learning technologies, human cognition, and emotional resilience could evolve in the harsh, exhilarating theater of space.

He was not alone. Alongside him aboard the Athena IX were two other scholar-astronauts: Dr. Selene Arroyo, whose research targeted neuroplasticity in Alzheimer's patients under microgravity, and Dr. Taro Okabe, a geologist-cartographer using orbital imaging to trace the outlines of ancient civilizations lost to time. Together, they were continuing a new model, educators as astronauts, scientists as content creators, and space as the ultimate classroom.

THE ATHENA IX
LEARNING POD: A
CLASSROOM IN ORBIT

The Athena IX shuttle, the crown jewel of multinational engineering, housed a gravity engine capable of producing short, Earth-like bursts of gravity. The Learning Pod, central to the mission, was designed in collaboration with Uwazi engineers to mirror the immersive experience of future learning environments:

- **Biometric Chairs**: Monitored vital signs, cognitive load, and emotional state during each session.
- **Haptic Feedback Desks**: Enabled tactile simulations of Earth-based activities in zero-G.
- **AR-Projection Domes**: Created immersive, 360-degree

visual environments with voice-activated instructional modules.

- **AI Tutoring Systems**: Modeled on Uwazi's culturally adaptive engine, responsive to user context and real-time behavior.

Each module could be streamed directly to Earth classrooms, labs, and professional training centers via ultra-low-latency communication channels, turning Athena IX into both a research station and a content studio.

EDUCATORS, PODCASTERS, AND EXPLORERS

The mission wasn't just collecting data. It was about connecting people. Ayo, Selene, and Taro each hosted their series of live-streamed podcasts and blogs, which were amplified through Uwazi's global learning platform and syndicated to schools, research institutions, and even public radio stations.

AYO'S LOG: THE ORBITING MIND

Ayo's podcast, titled The Orbiting Mind, explored educational philosophy, neurocognitive adaptation, and stories from students on Earth who were participating in live lessons. His most downloaded episode, "Learning Without Gravity," featured a floating book, bouncing markers, and a poetic discussion on how letting go—both literally and intellectually—can foster deeper engagement and curiosity. In space, you don't stand in front of the class. You float among ideas. – Ayo's Log, Episode 6

He also blogged daily, short reflections written during his orbital night cycle—quiet musings on perspective, vulnerability, and awe. A favorite among Earth readers was a post titled The Earth is a School Without Walls, which concluded with the line, From here, the borders are invisible and so are the limits we once believed in.

SELENE SPEAKS: GRAVITY OF MEMORY

Dr. Selene Arroyo's blog series, Gravity of Memory, combined neuroscience with narrative. In both video diaries and written posts, she documented her experiments on how microgravity affected the memory and neurochemical pathways of test subjects, some real-time Earth participants, others virtual. She also shared her emotional memories, triggered by smells, dreams, or the sight of Earthrise through the window. Her podcast became a quiet sensation among caregivers of Alzheimer's patients, praised for its intimate look at science through the lens of compassion. In microgravity, memories untether and float to the surface. It's not forgetting—it's rearranging. – Selene Speaks, Episode 3

CARTOGRAPHY OF SILENCE: TARO'S SEARCH FOR THE PAST

Dr. Taro Okabe's blog, Cartography of Silence, was part documentary, part speculative exploration. He released weekly updates featuring high-resolution overlays of suspected archaeological zones, including flooded coastlines, desert ridges, and lush rainforests. Using Athena's multi-spectral imaging, he believed he could identify anomalous formations, possible remnants of urban structures buried under centuries of sediment.

He also regularly interacted with high school geology clubs and university forums, offering students the opportunity to analyze and hypothesize using real-time data. One lucky group from Nairobi's Uwazi Academy even got to co-author a preliminary paper on terrain anomaly patterns in Madagascar's eastern coastline.

INTERACTIVE ORBIT: GLOBAL CONVERSATIONS FROM 200 MILES ABOVE

The Athena IX team wasn't broadcasting into a vacuum. Every stream, post, and lesson supported two-way interactions. The haptic desks, equipped with digital signature pads and remote-access interfaces, allowed students to feel the vibrations of a rocket launch, the weightlessness of space, and the texture of celestial bodies. Students could ask questions, send creative projects, or even pilot small learning simulations aboard the shuttle.

On one particularly moving day, a class of deaf students from São Paulo used sign language avatars in a state-of-the-art virtual reality pod, a part of the immersive learning environment of the Athena IX team, to ask Ayo: What does silence feel like in space?

His reply: It's a silence that lets you hear yourself, a unique sensory experience that only space can offer.

Meanwhile, Selene received messages from Alzheimer's families thanking her for humanizing the science. Taro mentored a cohort of young girls in Cambodia who were building DIY satellite models using Uwazi's open-source orbital simulation tools.

ECHOES OF HARMONY – CARMEL IN ACCRA

It was the third week of May, and the sidewalks of Washington, D.C., shimmered with late-spring heat. After weeks of final exams, papers, and long walks between dorms and lecture halls, Carmel MWendo-Joseph had officially completed her first year at Howard University. The city was alive with celebration: graduations, outdoor brunches, and the buzz of students packing up for summer. But for Carmel, summer would not begin with leisure.

She stood at the gates of Dulles International Airport with a carry-on slung over her shoulder and a fire in her chest. She was heading to Accra, Ghana, as part of the Uwazi Global Initiative for Young Entrepreneurs, joining a cohort of tech changemakers introducing their solutions across the African continent. Her mission: to support the official international launch of *Harmonic Code: Children on the Spectrum Composing Their Voice in Music*. It was more than a project. It was a personal symphony. A language she and her twin brother Caleb had composed from their own experience navigating life on the Autism Spectrum. Now, that melody was about to cross oceans.

The heat in D.C. that day was sticky and unpredictable, punctuated by sudden clouds and gusts of pollen-rich wind, classic mid-Atlantic weather. But as Carmel stepped off the plane in Kotoka International Airport 10 hours later, the change was immediate.

Accra in May was very humid, golden, and tropical, not oppressively hot but steady in its embrace at 84°F highs, 78°F lows. The coastal humidity wrapped around her like a silken shawl, and the air carried traces of salt, mango, and distant rhythms from open-air markets. In D.C., heat had meant exhaustion. Here, it felt cleansing, rhythmic, like a drumbeat marking the beginning of something sacred. Waiting for her outside baggage claim was Zen Chan, Uwazi's charismatic Chief Engagement Officer, dressed in light linen and a wide-brimmed hat. His smile widened as he spotted her. Carmel! Welcome to Accra, my radiant starlight. She grinned, adjusting her sunglasses. I don't know if I'm more excited or jetlagged. Both are forms of awakening, Zen said, linking arms with her. And we've got an orchestra waiting to tune.

They rode through the bustling streets of Osu in a community van branded with the Uwazi logo. It was 3 kilometers (1.9 miles) east of the central business district. Children waved from roadside kiosks, women carried baskets of fruit on their heads, and bright murals burst from concrete walls, each one a story painted in sunlight. In the van, Zen offered her a chilled bottle of coconut water and settled into his seat beside her. Do you remember the hackathon he asked about suddenly? Carmel looked out the window, the city's color melting into motion. I think about it from time to time. Caleb and I weren't even sure anyone would understand the idea. Music symbols and Leet speak? It felt niche.

Zen chuckled. It was genius. Unconventional, yes. But it wasn't about making people understand immediately. It was about giving children the tools to express themselves without forcing them to do it our way. He paused, then added more softly: The first time I heard a child in a pilot program *sing* their name using Harmonic Code, I cried. It was like hearing a heartbeat turn into a language.

Carmel swallowed hard. Her eyes watered, but it wasn't sadness. It was recognition. I think I cried the first time Caleb and I got the app to respond to a melody input. It was just a few notes, but the AI translated them back as a message: I'm here. That was it. I'm here. Zen nodded, eyes focused on the window, though his mind was replaying that moment with her. That message, he said, isn't just from the kids. It's from you and Caleb, too. That phrase I'm here is a declaration of presence and value. It's also, Carmel added with a quiet smile, an invitation.

THE LAUNCH

The next day, Carmel stood in front of Unity School for Neuro-diverse Learners, just outside Accra's central district. With her were Ghanaian educators, technologists, parents, and dozens of curious, eager children. They wore headphones and colorful badges printed with symbols from the Harmonic Code interface: ♩&, @.

As she demonstrated the app—playing short melodies and watching them turn into text, then voice- the children lit up. Some giggled, others quietly tested sequences. One boy composed a small tune and beamed as the AI translated his notes into My name is Kojo. I love drumming. By the end of the day, Harmonic Code was not a foreign tool. It was theirs.

That night, Carmel and Zen sat outside the guest lodge beneath a canopy of stars. The scent of roasted plantains lingered in the air. A drum circle echoed faintly from the neighboring community center. You know, Zen said, gazing upward, I used to think of innovation as something we push out into the world. But Harmonic Code? It's different. It pulls people in. Carmel exhaled slowly. I used to think Caleb and I created something to help kids like us. But now I see it's helping everyone *around* them learn how to *listen*. Zen clinked his glass of wine against her glass of coconut water, to liste*n* and to harmony. To Accra, Carmel added the beautiful noise of possibility.

In Ghana, Carmel was woken at dawn by a call from Ashanti. We're under attack, her mother said, her voice a strange blend of fire and fatigue. I need you to lead a community response circle with our legal youth fellows there. We need solidarity stories and public statements. Something human. Carmel, still in her pajamas, sat upright in bed. On it, mom. Carmie, Zen is already up to speed on the current situation. He will help you with how to proceed.

Carmie and Zen met to strategize on the approach to address the breach and cyber attack. By that afternoon, they gathered students, artists, and young lawyers for a livestream forum titled: Our Code, Our Culture: Voices from the Vanguard. They spoke not as victims, but as visionaries—describing what their innovations meant, why they mattered, and how digital spaces could hold both accountability and hope. Carmel closed the session with a call to action. Legacy speaks out loud and not in silence. In defense of each other, and we are not silent.

UNFORESEEN
COMPLICATIONS

Ashanti was in the middle of a late evening strategy call with Uwazi's Dakar team when her communications assistant's face flashed onto the screen, urgent and pale. Ma'am, there is an internal breach. The Nairobi Innovation Hub, hacked. The entire youth prototype archive was compromised and distributed openly online. Ashanti froze. Her body did not. End the call, she said sharply, switching to internal mode. Initiate Red Level Protocol. I want global team leads and cybersecurity on in ten. She muted her mic and closed her eyes for half a second—long enough to gather herself, short enough to remain steady. Ayo had once said: Leadership isn't about pretending to have control. It's about choosing who you become when control disappears. Now was one of those moments.

The next twelve hours were chaotic. A highly coordinated cyber-attack had targeted Uwazi's database and exposed dozens of unreleased youth-developed projects—some in testing, others deeply personal. AI poetry written by a Congolese refugee teen had gone viral without credit. A mental wellness app designed by girls in Kingston was being cloned for profit by a European tech firm. The Uwazi mission was built on radical trust and ethical tech. And now that trust was under siege. Media outlets were circling. Donors were calling. Uwazi's global credibility was cracking in real time. Ashanti hadn't slept in thirty hours. But she refused to retreat.

By midmorning, she was back in the Situation Room with the global team. Let's be clear, she said. The attack is intellectual theft and cultural violation, beyond a data leak. These young people trusted us. We owe them more than a cleanup—we owe them justice. The room nodded, digital and physical heads alike. Ashanti continued with a clear voice. We'll issue takedown orders. Launch a campaign to track the spread of stolen IP. But more importantly, we amplify the voices of those impacted. We will reclaim their work, which is not lost.

Across town, Caleb was at the youth hub when he got the alert.

He looked down at his wrist, eyes narrowing. He recognized one of the stolen projects; it was his. SoundSkin Beta 2.3, an emotional resonance patch, is now posted under a different name, already gaining views on a central content platform. For a moment, his stomach sank. Then he stood up, pulled his hoodie on, and called Jalen. We're not just pulling it down. We're going to show them who built it—and why that matters. They immediately started filming a digital rights PSA. No stylized edits. Just their faces, raw and direct. My name is Caleb MWendo-Joseph, he said into the camera. I'm not a credentialed engineer or corporate-funded developer. I'm a teenager living in D.C. who built something meaningful, and now it's being monetized by people who don't know my name. We're reclaiming it. Not just the code but the whole *story*. It went live within the hour. It spread faster than the stolen content.

Back in D.C., Ashanti stood in her office, watching the news. The narrative had shifted. Not because the breach didn't hurt, but because the response was collective, righteous, and visible. Donors recommitted. Journalists reframed. Young people around the world began using the hashtag #ReclaimReality. Ashanti sat back, her shoulders finally easing. The crisis wasn't over. But the momentum had returned to the right hands.

A knock on the door. Caleb stood there and asked, Do you have a minute? She nodded. He stepped in, holding up a sleek flash drive. SoundSkin 4.0. Not just reactive now. It *records* emotional data. Secure. Encrypted. Undeletable.

Ashanti blinked, impressed. He added, more quietly, I want to open source it. Name the youth who helped build it. No gatekeeping. Ashanti smiled. You've always had your path, she said. Now you're lighting it for others.

That night, with the brownstone finally quiet, Ashanti lit a candle in the corner of her room. The light was for what was lost, still to come, and would never be at risk again.

Three weeks had passed since the cyber breach at Uwazi. The quiet that followed was not relief; it was reconstruction for the data systems and a renewed sense of purpose. The internal review concluded that the breach came through a third-party platform used during a Nairobi-based innovation challenge. A line of insecure code had become a backdoor, opening months of youth work to theft. Swift actions taken include dropping the vendor immediately, with new security protocols implemented. But Ashanti knew: the real restoration wasn't technological. It was cultural. It was relational.

The Uwazi Resolution Forum, held simultaneously in D.C., Nairobi, Accra, Kingston, and virtually, marked a new chapter. Standing at the podium in a soft indigo suit, Ashanti addressed a global audience.

This crisis, she said, reminds us that legacy is beyond firewalls or funding; it requires trust. Trust is a living experience - when violated, we grieve. When honored, it multiplies.

Behind her, a new banner unfurled, bearing the words: Our Code. Our Culture. Our Collective Future. This phrase encapsulates our commitment to a shared set of principles, our dedication to nurturing a culture of inclusivity and innovation, and our vision for a future where our collective efforts lead to positive change.

New youth fellows, resilient and determined, were introduced, some of whom had previously been affected by the breach. Reparation grants had been issued. A global digital ethics curriculum, co-authored by students, was now required for all Uwazi teams. The organization would move forward differently and better.

Ashanti was transformed, not just as a leader, but as a woman. The crisis had forced her to lead from vulnerability, not just vision. To let her team see her tired, angry, afraid, and still faithful. She had learned to trust response over perfection. She no longer measured success by stability, but by adaptability. In the quiet, Ashanti re-centered Uwazi around four values: radical transparency, local ownership, story-first development, and co-creation over consumption. Her legacy was no longer just strategy; it was shared stewardship.

Caleb's voice now carried weight, not just among peers, but within Uwazi's strategy sessions. He'd been invited to co-lead the new Open Youth IP Collective, a platform dedicated to ensuring young creators worldwide retained legal and creative control of their work. This initiative, he believed, was a testament to Uwazi's commitment to empowering youth. He had learned that creativity was fragile but also fierce. He no longer rejected traditional systems; he now shaped alternatives. I used to think legacy was about proving something, he told a group of students at a youth summit. But now I think it's about protecting someone, including your future self.

Carmel returned from Ghana changed in posture, language, and conviction. She had seen the law weaponized. She had also seen it reclaimed. Now, she would finish her studies with a new mission: to build legal frameworks that treated youth ideas with the same dignity as corporate assets. She began working with a coalition of legal scholars and indigenous tech activists to design a Cultural Consent Protocol. A framework for safeguarding community-based innovations. She had learned that power wasn't just what you held. It was what you returned.

One night, back at the brownstone, the family gathered on the rooftop, no devices, just stars. Caleb leaned against the rail, eyes scanning the constellations. Carmel laid out candles in a quiet ritual she'd learned in Accra. Ashanti poured tea, her hands steady again. What now? Caleb asked, voice soft. Ashanti looked at each of them. Now we take a breath. We lead. We learn again. Carmel smiled and in a soft voice whispered, We remember. The night settled around them. Their futures were unwritten. But their foundations were firm. Together, through trial, truth, and tenacity, they had become a legacy in motion.

KATHY HAS
LEFT EARTH

On her final morning before treatment began in earnest, Kathy sat alone in her reading nook. The wind brushed the trees outside, and a single bird chirped persistently nearby. She wrapped herself in a thick shawl, reached for her cup of ginger tea, and smiled.

She looked not to the past, but forward—toward the undiscovered country of whatever came next. Let it begin, she said again, quietly, then she picked up her pen. She smiled to herself. *Let it begin.* She did not do her treatment. She collapsed and was able to press her medical alert emergency button before becoming unconscious. When emergency responders arrived, Kathy had left Earth.

They gathered under high arched ceilings and softened skylight in the Great Hall of the Uwazi Innovation Center—once designed to house world-changing ideas, today transformed into a sanctuary for remembering a world-changing woman.

Kathy Smith, visionary founder of Avant-Garde Metaverse and beloved Uwazi Fellow, had died peacefully in her sleep—her final days spent writing, mentoring, and leaving voice notes for the people she loved most.

Her final request was simple, yet sacred: Read the Seven Principles for Kingdom Living at my celebration. Speak of the God who anchored me, not the accolades that followed me. So they did.

Ashanti stood near the front, dressed in indigo and silver. Caleb and Carmel flanked her quietly, heads bowed, palms open on their laps. Ayo had sent his words days earlier—recorded aboard *Athena IX*, his voice cracked with emotion but certain in tone. His message played on a massive screen, the Earth slowly turning behind him in the background.

> Kathy, I once said your legacy would breathe without you. I see now I was wrong. Your legacy will soar. Higher than this orbit. Wider than any metaverse. You showed us that faith and code, healing and hardware, could coexist. You didn't just build technology—you built *testimony*. And I will carry your words with me, into the stars and back again."

The room fell into reverent silence. Ashanti rose and stepped forward, opening a folded parchment Kathy had signed just weeks before she passed. I was asked to read these words—not just for Kathy, but for us all, Ashanti said.

She began:

The Seven Principles for Kingdom Living

1. Love God, people, and yourself.
Love the Lord your God with all your heart, soul,

strength, and mind, and love your neighbor as yourself. *(Luke 10:27)*

2. Be Holy.
Be holy, because I am holy. *(1 Peter 1:16)*

3. Store up treasures in heaven.
But store up treasures for yourself in heaven, where moths and rust do not destroy. *(Matthew 6:20)*

4. Give generously.
For God loves a cheerful giver. *(2 Corinthians 9:7)*

5. Live by the Spirit of God.
The fruit of the Spirit is love, joy, peace, patience, kindness, goodness, faithfulness, gentleness, and self-control. *(Galatians 5:22)*

6. Let no debt remain but love.
Whoever loves others has fulfilled the law. *(Romans 13:8)*

7. Leave an inheritance for your children's children.
A good person leaves an inheritance for their children's children. *(Proverbs 13:22)*

Ashanti paused before folding the paper slowly. These were new principles to Kathy. She took them as her daily foundation. In her quiet wisdom, she wanted to share them with us, so we could receive the value she had gained from them.

The crowd was a mix of past and future.

Tarasi Richardson, head of product development, stood near the back with her team, red-rimmed eyes shining behind her glasses. She had brought Kathy's original headset design, now encased in crystal, placed at the foot of the lectern.

Marisela Rivera-Guzman, lead data scientist, held the latest iteration of the empathy model Kathy had once prototyped. She whispered to her colleague, Her code still runs.

Manny Pacquiao, COO, wore a white rose on his lapel and delivered a brief but heartfelt eulogy. Kathy was not only brilliant, he said. She was *brave*. Brave enough to believe technology could *heal*.

Zen Chan, chief engagement officer, led a communal silence—a timed three minutes of stillness—while one of Kathy's favorite soundscapes played softly. It was the recording of wind blowing through pines in the Japanese Alps, captured on one of her healing retreats.

Finally, Harry Reckenbacker, the current CEO of Avant-Garde Metaverse, approached the podium. We all stand on her shoulders, he said simply. We will never code, build, or lead the same way again.

Outside, as the sun began to set, attendees wrote messages on biodegradable lanterns shaped like VR lenses and released them into the sky. One by one, they floated upward, small lights chasing the horizon. Ashanti stood with Caleb and Carmel, arms linked. As the final lantern drifted out of view, Caleb whispered, She left a map. Carmel nodded. A mission. Ashanti closed her eyes. She left us with inspiration and a future. The rest we write.

Later that evening, Ayo hovered beside the port window aboard Athena IX, watching Earth's curve bathed in gold. He pressed his fingers to the recording interface one more time and whispered into the silence:

> Kathy has left Earth. But Earth hasn't left her. We will carry her here, where we teach, where we heal, where we build the next world together.

And with that, a soft tear floated upward into weightlessness.

ALMA'S WOMEN'S CIRCLE

You don't need to speak today. You can just be. – **Alma**

The scent of burning sage mingled with bergamot and fresh lime zest as the women entered the sunroom. Alma had laid soft woven rugs over the floor and arranged oversized cushions in a wide circle, sunlight pouring through the arched windows. A carved wooden bowl of sea glass, feathers, and handwritten affirmation cards sat in the center, surrounded by small tealight candles—each flickering with intention.

It was the second Sunday of the month. They came as they were engineers, doulas, public defenders, dancers, nurses, freelancers, mothers, daughters, newly-divorced, newly-arrived, newly-emerging from something heavy. The women's circle wasn't a support group. It wasn't therapy. It was a sanctuary. A space for women, especially those new to D.C. or navigating the aftermath of change, to pause, exhale, and speak without translation. Today, Ashanti was back.

She had missed the last two gatherings, first for the Uwazi crisis, then for Kathy's life celebration. As she entered, wearing soft denim and a long cream cardigan, Alma caught her eyes and opened her arms. No words. Just embrace. Ashanti held on longer than usual, her chin resting on Alma's shoulder, her body betraying the weight she hadn't spoken aloud. Alma pulled back and gently whispered, You don't need to talk today. You can just *be*. Ashanti nodded, her eyes already brimming.

The circle began with a grounding breath, led by Alma. They moved through gentle movement, then journaling prompts:

What truth have you been holding in your body that you haven't spoken aloud?
Who do you become when you stop performing strength?
What does healing look like now?

When it came time to share, Ashanti remained quiet at first. The other women's stories unfolded like petals—raw, unpolished, beautiful. One spoke of leaving a toxic job. Another aspect of rebuilding life after a miscarriage. Another step in learning to trust joy again after years of survival. Ashanti sat, listening, absorbing. Then, finally, her voice emerged—not forced, not performative, but trembling and true. I didn't realize how much I'd been holding until Kathy died, she began, eyes fixed on the flickering candles. She wasn't just a mentor. She opened my eyes so much ahead of me. She awakened many things I never knew I needed to believe in. The room quieted, honoring her. Ashanti continued, her voice soft. The world moves so fast, especially for women like us. We lead, we build, we carry. When we break, we're expected to break elegantly. A few women nodded, some closed their eyes. I've been grieving in fragments, she whispered. Between meetings. In bathrooms. On red-eye flights. But not like this. Not with women who know what it means to grieve while still keeping things running. Alma reached for her hand. You don't have to grieve in silence here. Another woman came forward, adding, or in solitude. Ashanti smiled through tears. Thank you.

At the end of the circle, Alma lit a single candle from the center and passed it to Ashanti. For who showed you your next horizon, she said. Ashanti held the candle close, heart aching and healing all at once. As the women hugged and lingered, exchanging numbers, offering rides, sharing herbal tea blends and playlists, Ashanti felt her shoulders lower. This was a re-rooting. In truth.

In softness. In sisterhood. When she finally stepped outside, the late afternoon sun warming her face, Ashanti knew: Grief would visit again. But so would grace. Alma's circle, this circle would always be there to catch her.

COACH MELODY
SUPPORT

Coaching sessions did not happen in an office. Never had. This time, it was a slow morning walk through Rock Creek Park. Melody traveled to be with Asdhanti in Ayo's absence. Let's start with this, Melody said gently, voice wrapped in velvet. What do you need now, in this moment, not as a CEO, not as a mother, not as Ayo's anchor, but just as Ashanti?

Ashanti paused, eyes blinking slower than usual. No one's asked me that in weeks, she whispered. I know, Melody said. Ashanti looked down at her hands. I think I need space to not lead just for a little while. Not to be the one who knows what to say. Melody nodded. Then let's not solve. Let's listen. What's waiting to be heard inside you? Ashanti inhaled. I haven't said this aloud before, but when Kathy died and Ayo was still in orbit, I felt like

I had no gravity. She was such a grounding force for me. He was my sky, and I was floating.

Melody leaned closer. That felt like what? Ashanti closed her eyes like drifting in deep water with no land in sight. I was still moving, still afloat but with no direction. Just reacting to waves. Wow, that's a powerful metaphor. Melody smiled softly. When the waves hit, what did you do? I kept working, Ashanti said. Held meetings. Showed up for the kids. Reassured donors. But inside, it was like there was a house full of rooms, and I locked the grief in the attic.

Melody let the silence stretch, sacred and unhurried. What if we opened that door today? she asked gently. Ashanti nodded slowly. Melody continued, When you think about Kathy now, not in her final days, but in your relationship, what stands out? She saw me, Ashanti whispered, even when I didn't say the right things. Even when I was exhausted, she could ask one question and disarm every defense. Like I just did? Melody said with a wink. Ashanti laughed through her tears, precisely like that.

They sat for a while longer, sifting through memory and meaning. Melody asked:
What have you been holding that no one has permitted you to put down?
Where have you been showing strength instead of seeking safety?
What would healing look like if it had a rhythm?

Each question drew Ashanti deeper, not toward solutions, but toward self-connection and truth.

As the session wound down, Melody's voice softened further. I've watched you build nations in your work, Ashanti. But remember, your soul is not a government; it does not need to perform stability. Ashanti placed a hand on her heart. I've missed you, she said. I'm always here, Melody replied as your coach, your sister, and the one holding the flashlight while you dig.

Ashanti wiped her eyes, smiling. Then help me find a new metaphor for this chapter. Not the floating one. Melody paused. How about this, what would be freeing for you? Ashanti started softly, I'm not floating anymore. I'm in a boat made of stories, and the water is the path, the oars are mine now. In excitement, she closes with, I get to choose what comes next. Ashanti exhaled. Oh wow, that feels true.

After they got back from the walk, Ashanti sat in the quiet of her home, no longer feeling lost at sea. The grief hadn't gone, but now it had formed. More importantly, it had company. Coach Melody had helped her return to herself. From that center, Ashanti knew that when Ayo came home, when Carmel left again, when the subsequent firestorm of leadership arrived, she would have something unshakable to return to herself.

AYO'S RETURN
FROM SPACE

He was supposed to be gone for thirty days. Just long enough to test learning systems in low-gravity environments, observe cognitive retention patterns, and report back on virtual classroom design in orbital conditions. But like so many journeys meant to be short, this one changed. A routine systems glitch turned into a cascading diagnostic failure across the Athena IX's atmospheric recalibration systems. The ship remained functional but with reduced redundancy, requiring every crew member to stay longer until the backup mission launched with parts. Ayo spent three months in space.

From orbit, Earth looked like a memory, beautiful, too far to touch. Time passed differently aboard *Athena IX*. Days were marked not by sunrises but by checklists. He taught classes remotely, reviewed youth curriculum simulations, and completed neuroplasticity reports. He recorded video messages for Ashanti, Carmie, and Caleb, each one more tender than the last. But silence crept in at night. Not the peace-of-mind kind. The bone-deep quiet that echoed too loudly.

He missed the weight of his wife's hand on his chest. He missed the thump of Caleb's bass-heavy beats from the other room. He missed Carmie's questions, rapid-fire and unfiltered. He missed being known beyond the mission. Still, he endured. He focused. He journaled. He prayed. Upon receiving the final transmission, the return schedule is as follows. Touchdown in six Earth days, he cried. No performance. No control, just relief.

Back on Earth, preparations for his return rippled through the MWendo-Joseph home like distant thunder. Ashanti hadn't said it aloud, but the delay had tested something sacred, her faith in time. Three months of parenting solo, managing global work, burying a friend, and recalibrating her mission. She'd hidden the fear well, even from herself. But when the launch window reopened, she exhaled for the first time in weeks. He's coming home, she whispered into the quiet. Carmie and Caleb each had their answers. Carmie set about preparing a photo slideshow of every significant life moment he'd missed. Caleb wrote a soundscape, a six-minute audio track built from archived samples of Ayo's voice messages, family recordings, heartbeat pulses, and the hush of atmospheric reentry. It was titled: Gravitational Return.

The capsule landed in the Mojave Desert late afternoon. The hatch opened slowly, a hiss of atmospheric reintegration. Crews helped the astronauts out one by one, bodies adjusting to gravity like newborns. Ayo stepped out, blinking under the desert sun, legs stiff, soul softer. Ashanti was there. The moment their eyes met, time collapsed. She didn't run. She walked. He didn't speak. He reached. In that long, anchoring embrace, three months of longing, doubt, and love rewoven itself. You're here, she whispered into his shoulder. I never really left, he replied.

RETURN AND RE-ENTRY: DEBRIEFING A PLANET

Upon return, the trio carried more than samples and readouts; they brought back an archive of interactive narratives, transdisciplinary insight, and lived experience. Their findings would go on to inform global learning strategy, therapeutic design, and space education curriculum. But perhaps the most significant achievement wasn't what they brought back; it was what they left behind:

> The first multi-modal orbital classroom is accessible to any school with a basic internet connection.

> A blueprint for inclusion in space exploration, proving that educators could be astronauts and content creators.

> A movement of global learning without borders, stitched together by orbit, empathy, and digital wisdom.

Ayo's muscles had atrophied. He moved slowly. Therapy sessions were scheduled daily, encompassing both psychological and physiological aspects. Rebuilding muscle, recalibrating balance, and confronting space-induced disorientation. Even with the fatigue and rehab routines, he insisted on family dinners. Long walks, even when they had to be short. Listening. Carmie told him about Ghana. Caleb shared his potential project with NASA's open innovation program. Ayo just smiled, eyes wet. You two are galaxies now. He shared stories of microgravity experiments gone wrong, the laughter of his crewmates, and the eerie silence of orbital night. But mostly, he listened. That was what space taught him: Presence is not proximity. Presence is attention.

Weeks later, at a Howard lecture hall packed beyond capacity, Ayo returned to the front of the classroom. Students stood when he entered. He held a simple object: a pen. This pen, he said, writes upside down, underwater, and in space. But it means nothing unless the hand holding it has something true to say. He paused. I left Earth to study the future of learning. What I found is this: wisdom is not upward. It is inward. It begins when we return to what matters. The audience erupted in applause.

That night, back at the brownstone, Ashanti joined Ayo on the porch under a sky filled with stars. Still dreaming about space?" she asked. He shook his head. I'm dreaming about us, how we keep making gravity together. They sat in silence, hands intertwined. Above them, the sky shimmered. But below, on Earth, everything important was already present.

Ayo returned to Earth with quiet eyes and a fuller heart. Space had been still, but his mind hadn't rested. The crisis back home had reached him mid-orbit. There was nothing he could do physically, but he had written a paper, Distributed Belonging: Learning Across Gravity, that wove his reflections on education in isolation with Ashanti's work on youth-powered justice. It will soon be published in Global Education Futures. His time above Earth helped him see that leadership wasn't a summit. It was generative. He was already planning a new course at Howard: Learning Beyond Borders. Ayo placed a small moon rock, his crew's gift to him, at the center of the table. We let the next generation build on what we leave behind. Ayo added.

THE NEXT STEP

The stage lights weren't bright. Intentionally designed to illuminate softly, without glare, casting an almost sacred glow on the circular panel at the center of the room. Ashanti adjusted her headset mic and looked out over the crowd, global thought leaders, youth activists, technologists, and village elders. This meeting was Ashanti's first appearance since Ayo's return, since the breach at Uwazi, since Kathy's passing. She didn't bring slides. She brought stories. When technology becomes more powerful than our memory, we must slow down, she began, her voice strong and clear. We must ask: Who holds the story of what we're building? More importantly, who will carry it forward?

A murmur of affirmation rippled through the crowd. Ashanti spoke of Uwazi's crisis and healing, mentorship, and loss. She centered her focus on the youth who code with rhythm, build from pain, and dream without permission. Then, she paused and pulled a folded slip of paper from her pocket, Kathy's hand-writing, preserved from the last letter Ashanti received before her friend transitioned. It read: Protect wonder. Guard memory. Build slowly. Walk with the ones who see. Ashanti raised her gaze. My next step is not just leadership, it's legacy stewardship. And I am no longer walking alone.

In a renovated textile factory in Accra, a crowd of Ghanaian high school students sat cross-legged in a circle, headphones on, immersed in a live podcast workshop. On the other side of the world, in a converted garage-turned-lab in D.C., another group of youth mirrored their posture, connected in real time.

Project EchoVerse has launched. Co-founded by Caleb and Carmel MWendo-Joseph, the initiative blended audio storytelling, wearable tech, and legal empowerment, training young people to produce immersive oral histories and protect their intellectual property from exploitation. Their pilot session was simple but powerful: What story does your body carry that the world needs to hear? Caleb managed the sensory integration system, each participant's voice tied to rhythmic biometric feedback, recorded and archived in a secure digital repository. Carmel facilitated the circle, guiding discussions with cultural sensitivity, legal frameworks, and a gentle, fierce presence.

One girl in Accra shared a lullaby her grandmother sang in Ewe, now encoded in an AI-protected file, titled only with her name. A boy in D.C. told the story of his neighborhood, using sound to map memories of grief and resilience. We call this street the heartbeat, he said. Because this is where we come back to. Every file closed with 'This is our code. Let no one rewrite it without us.'

Ashanti returned home late, the buzz of the summit still humming in her bones. She found Caleb and Carmel at the kitchen table, editing audio files and eating plantain chips from a communal bowl. She watched them for a moment, unnoticed, her children turned co-architects of the future. Still working?

she asked softly. Carmel looked up, eyes shining. We're launching the second cohort next month. Kigali and Oakland. Caleb added, We named the platform's archive The Smith Vault. However, Kathy would've liked that. Ashanti blinked back tears. She would've loved it.

They sat together, the three of them, scrolling through names, waveforms, raw clips of laughter, crying, protest chants, love songs, all stitched into the database like spiritual DNA. Ayo entered from the porch, pausing at the door. What are we building tonight? Ashanti turned, smiling. What's next for us?

THE INVITATION

The aroma of cinnamon-braised plantains filled the kitchen as Ashanti stirred a pot of okra stew on the stovetop, her brow glistening from the soft heat. Ayo poured hibiscus tea into a tall glass pitcher, and Caleb carefully laid out ceramic plates on the dining table. Tonight's guest was Jalen, Caleb's fast friend from Howard. Their connection had begun in a robotics lab over a stubborn AI bug and deepened through creative banter, late-night coding sessions, and shared dreams of using tech for social justice. Jalen had a gentle confidence, quiet and warm, yet anchored. He listened well. Asked better questions, when he spoke, even Ayo noticed the way his voice carried something was different, and he appeared rooted. Dinner was nearly ready when Jalen arrived. He offered Ashanti a bouquet of lilies and greeted Ayo with a respectful handshake, but his hug for Caleb was tight, brotherly, wordless. They discussed campus life, the VR mentorship app Carmel was developing, the upcoming Lunar

X Hackathon, and Caleb's fascination with rendering organic movement into robotics. Laughter bubbled. Even Uno and Duos curled under Jalen's chair, drawn to his calming presence.

Then, as the last bites of roasted sweet potatoes disappeared, Ayo leaned forward with a smile. Jalen, how are your parents doing? You mentioned visiting Brooklyn in the previous semester. The room shifted. For a beat, Jalen was quiet. He placed his fork down slowly, then lifted his eyes to meet Ayo's. He paused for a few seconds. I don't know my birth parents. Even Uno perked his head up. I was adopted, Jalen continued, voice even but soft—no paperwork trail. No names. It was a closed adoption. I was placed in the system early, bounced around a bit before I landed with a foster couple who raised me until I turned eighteen. I'm so sorry to hear that, Ashanti said gently, her hand resting lightly on the table. Jalen nodded with gratitude but didn't dwell there. It's all right. I was fortunate. I found a community through The Table Church. The men and women there mentored me. Taught me. Correct me. Encouraged me. I learned what it means to be an image bearer of God, not because of where I came from, but because of who I'm becoming.

The room was still. Not out of discomfort, but reverence. Caleb, did you know?" Carmel asked, her brow raised, voice almost a whisper. Caleb looked down, then at his friend. No, he said honestly. "We were always so caught up in building and innovating... we never got around to talking about where we came from. Jalen gave a small smile. Some of us are still figuring that out.

Jalen glanced around, sensing the weight his story had stirred. Hey, no pressure, he said, gently shifting the energy. But if you'd like, I'd love for you to come to church with me. Tomorrow morning. Just once. See for yourselves. Carmel answered before anyone else. I'd love to. Ayo and Ashanti chimed in, almost in unison: Yes, we would love to attend. Church starts at 10 a.m., Jalen added. We could meet at 9:30? Indeed, Carmel replied, her eyes already lighting with curiosity.

The next morning, the Joseph family arrived at The Table. The location was not prominent. Nestled between a community bookstore and a food co-op with no stained glass or organ pipes. Just wide, sunlit windows, folded chairs, exposed brick, and voices of every hue. The worship was soulful, bilingual, layered with harmonies of praise and spoken-word poetry. A violin played alongside a djembe. The congregation wasn't large, but it was diverse and spiritually present. Then the pastor stepped forward. She was striking, not because of her appearance, but her presence. Her voice rang clear but intimate, as if she were sitting in your living room instead of standing at a podium. Today, she began, we are going to talk about anointing—specifically, God's anointing of women in the church. Ashanti's eyebrows lifted. Carmel sat straighter. The pastor paced slowly. We begin with Sarah, Isaac's mother, whose laughter has become a lasting legacy. Then Mary, Jesus' mother, whose womb was the first altar of the New Covenant. However, we often overlook her cousin, Elizabeth, and the significance of prophetic community among women.

She paused, letting it settle. Then there's Mary Magdalene, a devoted follower of Jesus. Called a demon-possessed woman by tradition, but do you know who Jesus chose as the *first witness* of the resurrection? She let the silence speak. Not Peter. Not John. It was Mary. Whispers of agreement rippled through the sanctuary. What of Priscilla, who taught Apollos, a learned man of Scripture? Or the widow, the poor woman in Jesus' story, who gave two copper coins—*everything* she had. I call her Flo, because we don't even know her real name. Ashanti leaned in, eyes wide. The Bible's construction omitted many of these women, the pastor said. The Nicene Creed, formed under Constantine, emphasized order, but often at the cost of inclusion. Carmel turned slightly toward her mother and mouthed: Did you know that? Ashanti shook her head, eyes still on the pulpit. The sanctuary was hushed. No music. No clapping. No shifting in seats, just breath and silence. The pastor stood at the front of The Table

Church, her voice soft but ringing with quiet authority.

The choir began to sing, Walking in the Garden.

> I don't have to run
>
> I don't have to hide
>
> When we're walking in the garden
>
> When you call my name
>
> I won't be afraid
>
> When we're walking in the garden

The message had concluded. It had begun with scripture and expanded into fire, with testimonies from Mary and Priscilla, Sarah, and an unnamed widow, of faith wrapped in skin and silence, and sacrifice. The sermon had left a gap and an opening in the room. It lingered now like the final note of a hymn still vibrating in the soul.

Then the pastor spoke again. Suppose there is anyone here who desires prayer or feels the Spirit nudging you to explore what it means to walk with Jesus, not in religion or performance, but in relationship. In that case, the invitation is for you to stand. We would be honored to pray with you. You are not alone. You never were.

Her invitation floated into the room like a seed, then Ayo Josepho stood. He stood without a word. Without looking around for approval. Just calm and solid like a tree, remembering it once was a seed, too. Then he turned gently and extended his hand. Ashanti hesitated for just a breath. Her fingers hovered over his, unsure, unsteady, but she took it. She rose. Not as a woman who had all the answers, but as one willing to ask new questions. To be seen. To listen. To respond. Carmel watched her parents rise. Something inside her stirred. Not because of pressure, not fear, but a calling. The kind that didn't roar. It whispered. She stood too. Not because her parents did, but because something in her said: Your story is not just brilliance. It is a belief.

Caleb sat. His legs were frozen in place, and he was unwilling to move. His eyes fixed forward, his face unreadable. Around him, others rose. Some wept. Some smiled. Jalen stood too, head bowed, hands clasped in front of him. But Caleb remained still. He didn't feel resistance. He felt tension. The kind of tension that lives between logic and longing. Between wanting to understand and not being sure if he believed what he felt.

Caleb had always been the processor. The observer. He didn't rise because rising meant something. He didn't know what it was yet. But Jalen did not push. He didn't lean in or whisper or nudge. He simply turned, met Caleb's conflicted gaze, and with a steady voice, he said four words: The strength of women. The phrase struck like a soft chime inside Caleb's chest. Not in shame. But in recognition. His mind began to envision melodies of his mother, raising her voice in boardrooms full of resistance. Rhythms of Carmel, walking into college at sixteen like she belonged. The pastor's naming of Flo, the widow who gave everything and was known by no one, is a testament to the harmony. He thought of Mary Magdalene, the first to witness Jesus' resurrection. The strength of women. Those who carried the legacy silently. Who stood not to be seen, but to respond. Who rose, not when it was safe, but when it was sacred.

Still seated, Caleb closed his eyes. He didn't rise. Not that day. But he listened. In the quiet of his mind, a conversation began, not with the people around him, but with something within. Is it okay not to know? Yes. Is it OK to question? That's where wisdom begins. Do I have to believe like they do? No. But you do have to listen honestly. When the prayer concluded, Ayo and Ashanti embraced gently. Carmel's eyes were glassy but clear. Jalen wrapped his arm lightly around Caleb's shoulder. There was no rush. No pressure. No judgment. Just presence. For Caleb, that was enough.

The Josephs left slowly, each bearing the weight of what they had just heard. Outside, birds chirped in rhythm with passing cars, and the air was crisp with late-spring clarity. That message, Ashanti said, is still being processed. I had no idea how many women were silenced by historical interpretation. Flo, Carmel whispered. She matters too. Her two coins still echo. They all stood in quiet reflection for a moment longer. Then Jalen turned to them. What did you think? I think Caleb said slowly that The Table is more than a church. It's a classroom. Today, we got enlightened.

On the way back to Kalorama, no one pushed for conversation. The air was full but soft. The family sat in what Carmel started to sing the words to Walking in the Garden. 'When you call my name, I won't be afraid, When we're walking in the garden.' She would later write in her journal of a sacred stillness. Ashanti reached over and squeezed Caleb's hand. You okay, baby? Yeah, he said. I'm just thinking. Ayo glanced at him in the rearview mirror and nodded. That's how most awakenings start.

That evening, Ashanti lit a candle on the kitchen counter, something she hadn't done in weeks. Not for mood or scent, but intention. To Flo, she whispered. To all the women the world forgot but heaven remembers. Carmel picked up a pen and wrote Flo in the margin of her journal, then added: Faith lives where stories told change lives. Upstairs, Caleb was sketching again. This time, it wasn't robotics. It was a simple image: a copper coin resting in a woman's hand, and beneath it, the outline of a world turning. Somewhere inside, a new kind of treasure was being stored, not in gold, but in truth.

Caleb opened his tablet. He drew a field, open and wide. Soft winds move through the grass. In the distance, a tree half-bloomed, roots visible beneath the earth, stretching outward like questions. At the base of the tree stood three figures, tall, radiant, unmoved by the wind: his mother, his sister, and a woman with no name, holding two copper coins. In the corner, he wrote: I didn't stand. But I saw them. Maybe that's where standing begins.

THE DISINFORMATION WAR

They tried to rewrite me, but I've got my pen. – **Carmel**

It started with a whisper. A forty-seven-second clip surfaced on a fringe political video platform, showing Carmel and Caleb MWendo-Joseph, polished and poised, standing behind a podium with an eagle insignia. In unison, they praised the "firm leadership" of the President of the United States. The same president whose policies had torn apart immigrant families, gutted social aid programs, and stoked fear with every press conference. We stand for America first, Caleb's voice said, mechanical but familiar. No more wasting aid on foreign nations while Americans suffer, Carmel added. We renounce Uwazi's international ambitions, they said together. A still image closed the clip—Carmel smiling beside a red-white-and-blue flag, Caleb raising a fist. It spread like wildfire.

Within hours, it had reached millions of views. Another video dropped, this one more aggressive. Carmel, her image crisp and convincing, sang a modified version of America the Beautiful with lyrics slandering asylum seekers. Caleb, eyes blazing, called social assistance a crutch for the lazy. Ayo watched the second video in horror, the laptop glowing against his face in the early morning dark. Ashanti burst into the room, her phone vibrating with messages from media contacts, Howard faculty, and Uwazi board members. Turn it off, she said, her voice cracking. Please, Ayo, turn it off. It's not them, he whispered, almost to himself. It's *not them*. But the internet didn't wait for verification. By noon, international news outlets had picked up the story. #TwinsOfTreason and #UwaziTraitors were trending on social media. Activists in Ghana and South Africa denounced the Mwendos. Political pundits celebrated the "surprising shift" in Gen Z politics. The damage was real, and it was growing.

The Uwazi headquarters in D.C. was a blur of activity. Tarasi Richardson, head of product development, had stopped mid-sprint of an accessibility prototype and rerouted her engineering team. Marisela Rivera-Guzman, the lead data scientist, pulled her machine learning analysts into the war room. Manny Pacquiao, the ever-calm COO, issued an internal red alert, shutting down Uwazi's external social media feeds, initiating protocol for reputational crises, and escalating to legal action. Zen Chan was already speaking live on a community radio show by 7:15 a.m., voice steady. The Josephs did not say these things. The videos are fabrications. Deepfakes. The cyber attacks target their family and the ideals they represent. But they *look* real, the host said. So did the Trojan Horse, Zen replied.

By nightfall, Ashanti sat silently on the couch, hands clasped tight, her foot bouncing uncontrollably. Coach Melody arrived just after 9:00 p.m., her suitcase still in the Uber. A regal presence in a long wool coat, she entered the Mwendo home like a shield. You look exhausted, Melody said gently, settling beside Ashanti. I'm worse than exhausted, Ashanti admitted. I'm wounded. Melody reached over, placed a warm hand on hers. Then we heal. But first—we fight smart"

Melody, a renowned executive coach specializing in the resilience of African American women in leadership, had come armed with more than empathy. She had networks. Tools. Language. She'd grown up in Oregon, but her roots stretched into Black Southern resistance, and her presence reminded Ashanti of all the women who had held lineages together with prayer, strategy, and fire.

Upstairs, Caleb and Carmel sat in Carmel's room, still in shock. How could they fake our voices? Carmel asked. They trained on public data, Caleb muttered. Our TEDx talk. Podcasts. Interviews. But what do we *do*? Caleb didn't answer.

Back at Uwazi HQ, Tarasi and Marisela initiated the Sentinel Protocol. They had anticipated a day like this, ever since synthetic media had crossed the uncanny chasm. Now, it was real, targeted, and personal. Their solution: build bots to fight bots. Using pattern recognition models, the team reverse-engineered the architecture of the deepfake generators. They trained defensive AIs, called Echo and Coda, to scour the web for instances of manipulated audio and visual fingerprints. It was a digital dogfight. Every time we take one down, Marisela mutters, eyes red from screen glare, three more sprout like Hydra heads. Then we evolve faster, Tarasi said, tying her locs into a bun. We didn't build Uwazi to be passive. Harry Reckenbacker, CEO of Avant-Garde Metaverse, called Ashanti directly. I just want you to know, he said, his voice rough but sincere, if these were *my* kids, you'd be here for me. We're under siege, Ashanti said flatly. Then let's dig in, he replied. My R&D division is yours. Use all of it.

Coach Melody worked with Ayo and Ashanti to prepare a statement, not defensive, not corporate, but deeply human. They released it on every channel:

> We are parents to Carmel and Caleb MWendo-Joseph. Our children—two sixteen-year-olds devoted to education, empathy, and global equity—are being used as pawns in a campaign of disinformation. The content circulating is false. Fabricated. Cruel. But this is more than about us. The aim is about the soul of truth in a digital age. We will not be silent or erased. We will rise, not in fear, but in fire.

The statement caught fire. Prominent voices in tech, education, and civil rights responded with support. Faith leaders issued prayers. Ghanaian activists withdrew their condemnation and demanded global regulation on deepfakes. The tide had shifted. But it was not over.

Inside Uwazi's digital ops room, Echo and Coda were evolving. One bot embedded itself in dark web threads, poisoning deepfake networks with false-positive markers, which led to their systems crashing. Another began creating hallucinated artifacts, fake fakes, to confuse and destabilize the algorithms spreading the videos.

It was a cyberwar of nuance, fought in milliseconds and terabytes. It's like the Matrix, Caleb whispered to Carmel as they watched real-time data visualizations blink and blur. But we're not dodging bullets. We're dodging false versions of ourselves. They tried to turn us into villains, Carmel said, eyes sharp. But we're still here. Not just still, Caleb said. Stronger.

Coach Melody, in collaboration with Ashanti and Zen, hosted a virtual town hall. Over 30,000 people joined. They titled it: The Digital Weaponization of Identity: Fighting for Our Stories in the Age of Deepfake Propaganda. Ashanti delivered the keynote. Her voice was steel. These acts aren't just a political tactic. It's a cultural assault. It targets the voices of color, dissent, and innovation. It seeks to discredit by distortion. But we will not yield. We will not let artificial lies overwrite ancestral truth. She ended with Carmel and Caleb by her side. These are my children. I know their character, their hearts, their dreams. Algorithms don't know what I know. But I will teach them. The chat exploded in support.

By the end of the week, Echo and Coda had neutralized 93% of circulating deepfakes. Public sentiment had shifted firmly in favor of the Mwendos. Major outlets ran follow-up exposés titled:

> Deepfake Nation: The Digital Lynching of the MWendo-Joseph Twins
> Synthetic Lies, Real Harm: How One Family Fought Back

But healing would take time. Ashanti began therapy. So did Caleb. Carmel resumed her journal. Ayo started writing a memoir, not for fame, but to archive the truth. Coach Melody stayed through the weekend. On Sunday night, they lit candles and just breathed. As the flames flickered, Ashanti whispered, I miss decency. Melody nodded. Then we build it back. One truth at a time.

Carmel's Journal – The Week We Were Rewritten

Day One
Title: Blur

It doesn't even *sound* like me. It looks like me. Smiles like me. But the eyes are hollow. I've watched it twelve times. That awful clip. Twelve. Each time, something in my chest becomes colder. Not because I think it's true, but because I know someone else does. Millions of someone else's, and I can't stop them. I can't reach the screen and retreat. It's strange. I've always loved tech. I loved the logic. The beauty of pattern. The wonder of what *could* be. But now I wonder what happens when people weaponize code against character. Caleb hasn't said much. He's been typing all day with earbuds in. Face locked. I think he's trying to build something. A shield, maybe. Meanwhile, I'm trying to feel my name again.

Day Two
Title: Flameproof

Ashanti, we're not allowed to call her "Mom" when she's in warrior mode—standing in the living room like an anchor today. She said: I've spent my life making sure my babies were protected. But now they're grown enough to be targeted. She said it like a prayer and a warning. I didn't cry.

Not when I saw the hashtags. Not when a so-called journalist called me a traitor to Pan-Africanism. Not even when a girl I knew DM'd me: You're disgusting. But when Ayo walked into my room with a bowl of mango slices and said, I know who you are, I almost broke down. Almost. Coach Melody arrived tonight. She smells like sandalwood and power. I like her already.

Day Three
Title: The Matrix Is Real

Caleb, let me watch the Uwazi ops dashboard today. There are *bots* fighting bots. Little digital armies flying through the internet, identifying deepfake distortions, infecting hostile nodes, faking fakes to confuse malicious networks. It's beautiful, Marisela calls them Echo and Coda. It feels like watching neurons fire in real-time. But instead of thoughts, they're defending my *face*. The bot war is what the future looks like, I guess. However, we will pursue truth in code, lift our voices in exile, and find redemption in a binary world. Still, I want to scream. Not because I'm afraid, but because I'm tired of *always* having to prove I'm real.

Day Four
Title: Flo

We watched our family's video statement today. I looked so calm. I don't remember being calm. I remember being furious. Zen said people are starting to believe us again. That the tide is turning, but some stains don't come out. I've read the comment sections. I shouldn't have, but I did. Someone said, If she were innocent, she would have cried.

Someone else said, They're just trying to backpedal because they got caught. What do you do when the lie is louder than your truth? You whisper it again. And again. Until it breaks through, I wrote "Flo" in the back of this journal today. The widow from scripture. Two copper coins and no name. History forgot her. But heaven didn't.

Day Five
Title: Caleb's Quiet

He finally talked to me. We sat on the floor of my room, eating peanut butter straight from the jar. They took our voices, he said. Now we build new ones. He's been sketching again. I peeked. One drawing had three versions of me. One made of pixels. One made of wires. One made of stars. He called it: Carmel, Recompiled. I hugged him so hard I think I cracked his spine.

Day Six
Title: Still Here

Coach Melody led us in a breathing exercise this morning. Said, the world will try to delete you. So inhale like you're making yourself undeniable. So I did. I went outside without sunglasses for the first time all week. Head up. Shoulders loose. Two people recognized me. One crossed the street. One nodded. I nodded back. Later, we had a candle circle. The coach lit seven flames. One for each day since the storm began. When the coach lit my flame, I said nothing. But I thought: I'm still here, still real, and I still believe in light.

Day Seven
Title: New Code

The videos are almost gone. Echo and Coda are winning. Tarasi says Uwazi's going to open-source the protocol. Let others fight their digital wars. I told her she's a legend. She just winked. Zen hugged me today. The real kind. Not the polite Chief Engagement Officer hug, but a soul-anchoring hug. Ashanti cried during dinner. Ayo toasted with ginger beer and said, To tell you the truth. And to the kids who defended it. I don't know what will come next. I don't know who still believes the lie. But I know who I am.

I am not synthetic, not shallow, and certainly not shaken.

I am the daughter of Ashanti and Ayo. I am the twin of Caleb, who codes truth into being. I am a storyteller, a system-breaker, and a solid revolution in real skin.

They tried to rewrite me, but I've got my pen.

—Carmel

UWAZI AND AVANT-GARDE METAVERSE SUCCESSFULLY NEUTRALIZE GLOBAL DEEPFAKE ATTACK

FOR IMMEDIATE RELEASE
Date: November 10, 2025

Contact:
Zen Chan, Chief Engagement Officer, Uwazi –
media@uwazi.global
Dr. Lyla Kwon, Director of Communications, Avant-Garde
Metaverse – press@avantgarde.io

Joint Tech-Human Defense Protocol Restores Truth and Reclaims the Identities of Targeted Youth Innovators

Washington, D.C. — In response to a malicious deepfake campaign targeting Uwazi ambassadors Carmel and Caleb MWendo-Joseph, Uwazi and Avant-Garde Metaverse have successfully neutralized over 93% of harmful digital content propagated through artificial video manipulation systems. The deepfake materials falsely depicted the Mwendo twins endorsing authoritarian policies and denouncing their humanitarian work with

Uwazi.

The joint technical response, codenamed Operation Sentinel, deployed a novel anti-deepfake architecture developed in real time by Uwazi's in-house machine learning and digital ethics teams, with full support from Avant-Garde Metaverse's immersive AI research division.

> The attacks were more than a reputational crisis; it was an attack on truth, youth, and justice, said Tarasi Richardson, Head of Product Development at Uwazi. We didn't just defend two brilliant teenagers, we defended the integrity of public discourse in the age of synthetic manipulation.

A NEW DIGITAL DEFENSE STANDARD: ECHO + CODA

Central to the success of Operation Sentinel were two AI defensive systems developed by Uwazi and open-sourced with support from Avant-Garde Metaverse:

> **ECHO**: A real-time fingerprint-matching system capable of detecting and neutralizing manipulated audio-visual assets across platforms within seconds of upload.

> **CODA**: A strategic counter-narrative engine that floods misinformation nodes with simulated deepfakes, disrupting algorithmic amplification and discrediting attacker reliability.

This is what partnership looks like, said Harry Reckenbacker, CEO of Avant-Garde Metaverse. These weren't just tech solutions. They were acts of protection and solidarity. If these were my kids, I know Uwazi would have shown up. That's what we did—and will keep doing.

A MESSAGE FROM THE JOSEPH FAMILY

Dr. Ayo Joseph and Dr. Ashanti MWendo, parents of Carmel and Caleb, released the following statement:

> We are grateful beyond measure for the coordinated campaign to silence the voices of young leaders shaping a just, interconnected world. Thanks to Uwazi, Avant-Garde Metaverse, and the global community that stood with us. We are not only restored, but resolved. We will not be intimidated. We will continue to build.

CALL TO ACTION: DIGITAL JUSTICE IN THE AGE OF DEEP-FAKES

Uwazi and Avant-Garde Metaverse will host an international summit on Digital Sovereignty and Synthetic Ethics in Fall 2025. The summit will convene public leaders, educators, technologists, youth innovators, and policymakers to establish a universal digital bill of rights and ethics framework for synthetic media.

> This is the beginning of a new digital human rights movement, said Zen Chan, Uwazi's Chief Engagement Officer. We're calling on governments, NGOs, and tech companies worldwide to protect the right to be real.

ABOUT UWAZI

Uwazi is a global social innovation venture that connects immersive learning, community transformation, and youth leadership. Its programs span four continents, integrating emerging technology with ancestral wisdom to drive inclusive education and economic empowerment.

ABOUT AVANT-GARDE METAVERSE

Avant-Garde Metaverse is a pioneer in virtual reality and augmented human experience, dedicated to building ethical, accessible, and transformative technologies. It is a longtime ally in the fight for digital inclusion and narrative sovereignty.

For further information or partnership inquiries, please contact:
press@uwazi.global | media@avantgarde.io
www.uwazi.global | www.avantgarde.io

THE EFFECT OF COACHING ON THE HUMAN SPIRIT – COACH MELODY ON STAGE

I don't fix people. I walk with them. I remind them. I help them hear the silenced part of themselves. – **Melody**

The studio lights were bright, but not blinding. Coach Melody Ellison, wrapped in a deep plum pantsuit, stood at the center of a polished stage, palms open, her breath measured, her presence magnetic. The room was silent, not out of politeness, but anticipation. Behind her, the unmistakable banner read: Super Soul Sundays: The Human Spirit Series – Hosted by Oprah Winfrey. She hadn't come seeking fame. But now, standing before a global audience, she was there to do what she'd always done: hold space for truth to rise.

The invitation came two weeks after the televised crisis surrounding Carmel and Caleb MWendo-Joseph. Coach Melody had flown to D.C. not as a consultant, not as a strategist, but as a sister-friend to Ashanti MWendo, a woman bearing the weight of the world, two children under attack, a company under pressure, a husband preparing for space. Melody had known Ashanti since the days when they were the only two Black women in a venture capital cohort in Silicon Valley. Their bond had grown from mutual respect into covenant.

Melody didn't swoop in with fix-it answers. She listened. She guided me. She asked the questions no one else could ask, and then held Ashanti's hand while she found her own. You don't have to be steel all the time, Melody had said that first night in Kalorama. But I do, Ashanti whispered. I'm a CEO. A mother. A symbol.
Symbols are static, Melody said. But you're alive. Let's start there.

The clip had gone viral. A behind-the-scenes moment during a Uwazi town hall, Ashanti turns to hug Coach Melody after a powerful keynote about reclaiming narrative. The embrace was brief, but the camera caught something raw: a global leader melting into the arms of her coach, her sister, her anchor.

Oprah's producer called three days later. We watched that moment a dozen times, she said. It wasn't what Ashanti said; it was how she leaned into you. We want to explore that. We would like to discuss the impact of coaching on the human spirit. Will you come?"

Melody hesitated. She didn't crave cameras. But she *did* crave awakening. I'll come, she said. But only if we discuss everything.

The mothers. The daughters. The executives. The silence we swallow. The rise that hurts.

Now, she stood under lights once reserved for heads of state and Grammy winners.

Oprah welcomed her with open arms. We're honored to have Coach Melody Ellison with us today. She's not just a coach, she's a catalyst, a presence. And as the world recently witnessed, she is the quiet behind the strength. Melody nodded graciously. I don't fix people, she began. I reflect on them. I remind them. I help them hear the part of themselves silenced by responsibility.

Oprah leaned in. You helped Ashanti MWendo, one of the most recognized global CEOs of African descent, through one of the most challenging weeks of her life. What did you offer her?"

Melody paused. Permission. The audience sat with the word. Ashanti is a world-builder. But even architects need rest. Even warriors need sanctuary. Coaching, at its core, is spiritual architecture. I didn't give her strength. I helped her *see* the strength she'd been hiding under leadership armor. What about her children?" Oprah asked. Carmel and Caleb? Melody smiled. They reminded me why this work matters. When the world tried to redefine them with synthetic lies, their *essence* stayed intact. That's the fruit of parenting that centers presence, not perfection.

Melody turned to the audience. Coaching is not a trend. It's not a productivity hack. It's a mirror, a moment of reverence. When done with integrity, it becomes a spiritual intervention. She shared how her coaching found form growing up in Oregon. The only Black girl in the room, again and again, and by listening to the ancestral whispers of her Southern elders. My grandmother used to say, You can be heard without raising your voice. You raise your *presence*.' Coaching is how I teach presence.

As the show neared its end, Oprah asked: What would you say to every woman watching today who's trying to hold everything together? Melody looked directly into the camera. Let go of the myth of having it all. We are more than a brand. We are not machines. I witness people seeking balance in life. But we are here to *be* whole, to be seen, to be held, and to be human. Let someone walk with you. Find your mirror. Find your coach. If you can't find one, be one for someone else. A silence swept the room. Oprah closed her notebook slowly. That wisdom was a moment in church. The audience stood. Applause erupted. But Melody remained still and anchored in radiance. Backstage, Melody received a quiet text from Ashanti: I watched, wept, and I remember now. Thank you, Sis.

Then, another from Carmel: I want to develop coaching skills as I grow up. That's the real superpower. Melody smiled and hid her phone. Coaching, she knew, didn't always make headlines. But today it had. It had done so not with soundbites, but with soul.

THE SEARCH FOR JALEN'S FAMILY

The rain had just stopped. Carmel leaned against Caleb's doorframe, her curls damp with drizzle, the scent of petrichor clinging to her hoodie. His room was quiet, save for the soft hum of his laptop and the tap-tap-tap of his keyboard. She watched him for a moment. It was familiar, his focus on the task at hand.

Then she said it softly, as if the question might float away if said too loudly. Do you think God could help us find Jalen's birth family? Caleb didn't look up immediately. He typed for a few more seconds. Then paused. Fingers suspended in the air. What made you ask that question?

Carmel stepped into the room and sat cross-legged on the floor, knees brushing the corner of his bed frame. I don't know. I was thinking about the message at The Table church. The one about Sarah and Mary and the widow, you remember? Yeah, he nodded. The one where the pastor named the women left unnamed by history. Right, she said. It made me think Jalen's story is still in motion. Maybe God could do something unexpected.

Caleb exhaled thoughtfully, then finally met her gaze. I believe miracles are possible, he said. But I also believe in machine learning. Facial recognition. Genealogical mapping. Public records databases. If there's a trail, our AI could find it. Carmel tilted her head. Do you trust code more than God? He gave a half-smile. I trust what I can work with. AI isn't invisible. It doesn't need belief to function. But maybe God does, she replied.

They were twins, but not carbon copies. Carmel lived by feeling. Songs and symbols. Dreams and devotion. Caleb lived by logic. Syntax and structure. Numbers that added up. Both were right in their unique ways. At this moment, both were reaching for Jalen. He'd never asked them to find his birth family. He'd rarely spoken of them, just that he was adopted. He also said the Table church had raised him, and he was grateful. But Carmel had seen the flicker in his eyes whenever someone mentioned roots. She saw it even when Jalen didn't know he was showing it—the wonder of legacy, a mother's name, or a father's face. Their journey was a rollercoaster of emotions, a testament to their love for Jalen.

That night, Caleb began quietly building a search model. He didn't announce it. He opened a fresh Jupyter notebook and began creating a framework:

- Input: DNA database matching (voluntary)
- Cross-reference: Open adoption registries
- Filter: Geographic proximity to early adoption records
- Output: Probable matches, descending confidence levels

Meanwhile, Carmel opened her journal. She began writing a letter, not to Jalen or herself, but to God.

Dear God,
If you're listening—and I think you are—I want to find Jalen's family. Not because he needs fixing. But because he deserves to know. He deserves history. And maybe healing. If Caleb finds them through AI, fine. But if you see them through grace, it's better. Amen.

Then she began humming a tune from the Table church service:

I don't have to run, I don't have to hide, when we're walking in the garden.

The next morning, Carmel found Jalen near Howard's Reflecting

Pool, sitting on a bench. She didn't mention the search. Instead, she sat beside him, let the silence settle, and hummed again. That song, he said softly. Do you remember it? She smiled. Yeah. From our visit to the Table church. When my family and I stood for the altar call, Caleb didn't join us. Jalen looked at her and said One day, when God is ready for him. She turned to him. Maybe one day.

In the days that followed, Caleb's AI model began populating potential leads. Unconfirmed. Inconclusive. But it is possible. Carmel, on the other hand, started organizing a small prayer circle at The Table. She didn't tell Jalen what it was for, not yet. Two paths. One hope. The uncertainty of the outcome hung in the air, adding a layer of suspense to their journey.

Technology and Spirit walk parallel lines toward the same garden. In between it all, Jalen was unaware that a search had begun. Unaware that two people loved him enough to chase both science and soul for his sake. Their determination was unwavering, inspiring those around them.

That night, Carmel stood by her window, whispering the melody once more, this time adding her own words to the song.

> Walking in the garden, holding onto peace, I don't need the answers, just a little light for me to see

Behind her, Caleb typed the last line of his search model's code: **return trace_lineage(Jalen).

They didn't know which path would lead first. They both believed now. The search had begun.

FINDING ROOTS,
FINDING TRUTH

It was a soft, golden Sunday in Kalorama. The kind that smelled of cinnamon bread and budding magnolias. Jalen had accepted Carmel's casual invite to brunch at the Mwendo home, just as he had a dozen times before. He didn't suspect anything. Why would he? Carmel and Caleb always invited him, whether it was for weekend waffles, new jazz records, or backyard debates about whether AI or human intuition would win in a crisis. But this Sunday, something more was stirring. Ashanti had set the table with mismatched vintage dishes and warm sweet potato hash. Ayo had prepared his signature ginger-spiced tea. Uno and Duos circled the table like tiny sentinels of joy. Caleb, quiet, observant, steady, was carrying the weight of a choice. Because today was the day he would collect Jalen's DNA.

It started as a conversation. Carmel nd Caleb spent time developing a shared idea. Then came the mission. We don't need to tell him yet, Carmel had said softly. Not if there's nothing to tell. If there is something to tell, Caleb added, we'd be ready because we'd know. If you do this, let love, not curiosity, guide you.

So they prepared carefully. Carmel ordered an FDA-approved DNA collection kit. Caleb integrated it with the *Finding Your Roots* intake system, knowing that the database built by Dr. Henry Louis Gates, Jr., could parse lineages that most platforms couldn't handle. All they needed was a sample.

During brunch, Jalen reached for his glass of sparkling hibiscus water, took a few sips, and then leaned back into a conversation about Ghanaian beat cycles and their influence on Afrofuturist soundscapes. When he excused himself to go to the bathroom, Caleb quietly slid the glass into a zippered collection pouch. He labeled it Guest 0423 – J.M. At first, Caleb saw this act of secrecy as espionage. Carmel convinced him it was intercession. Carmel boxed the sample for overnight delivery to the Gates Lab's genealogical network. She whispered a short prayer over the box: Let this reveal what love could not reach before.

That night, Caleb sat on his bed in the dark, thinking. Did I cross a line? How would I feel if my friend and sister did this to me?. He also considered what it felt like to wonder who you came from, and what silence could do to a boy who never had a mother's name or a father's face.

The match came ten days later. In the results, Jalen's mother's name and the city he was born in were listed; there was history, and for Caleb and Carmel, a responsibility. They knew now, and with that knowing came the burden of telling Jalen not just that he came from somewhere. But there is a redemption story of how I was once lost, but now I am found. After they revealed the discovery to Jalen, a moment of dense quiet fell between them. The kind that makes time stand still. Then Jalen asked: Did I give you my DNA? Carmel looked down. No, she said, you didn't. We collected it during brunch from your glass. His jaw tightened slightly. But his eyes became moist with tears. You two went all-in on this? Yes, Caleb said. We didn't want to violate your trust. We only wanted to help you find *yourself.* Jalen looked at them for a long time, then chuckled dryly. I thought I was the tech nerd. Then came the slow nod. Okay. I'm not mad. But I *am* overwhelmed. We can sit with that, Carmel said, as long as you need. Later that night, Jalen texted Carmel and Caleb one line: I forgive the method. I received the message, beneath it: *#FindingMyRoots #Fo.rAkua.*

JALEN ON FINDING YOUR ROOTS

To every kid who doesn't know where they came from, you are valuable. You are becoming, and sometimes, finding your roots means letting someone else water the soil. – **Jalen**

The letter had come two weeks after the DNA match. A crisp envelope bearing the seal of the W.E.B. Du Bois Institute for African and African American Research at Harvard.

Inside, an invitation:

Dear Jalen,
Your story has deeply moved our team. We would be honored to include you in an upcoming special episode of Finding Your Roots entitled Children of Silence: Reclaiming the Lineage of the Lost. Your journey is not only personal, it is generational.
Please say yes.

Warmly,
Dr. Henry Louis Gates, Jr.

The lights weren't too bright. They were warm, even cinematic, the kind that made brown skin glow and stories unfold like sunrises. Jalen sat upright in the studio chair, his fingers laced together, his eyes focused just beyond the camera, where Dr. Henry Louis Gates, Jr. sat poised with a gentle smile and a thick folder in his hands. The logo shimmered on the monitor behind them:

FINDING YOUR ROOTS
With Henry Louis Gates, Jr.

Jalen exhaled slowly. He could still feel the pulse of his heart in his throat, but he was ready.

Dr. Gates opened the conversation warmly, his voice like jazz: smooth, intelligent, alive with rhythm. Jalen, when we began researching your family, we weren't sure where the trail would lead. But what we uncovered is profound. He opened the folder. Your mother, Akua Nkrumah, was born in a fishing village just outside Accra, Ghana. She was the daughter of a schoolteacher and an herbalist. Bright. Curious. Artistic. A photo slid into view. It was her. Jalen's eyes widened. She was beautiful. Eyes like his. Brow just slightly arched. A quiet defiance in her smile.

Dr. Gates continued. She came to the U.S. on a student visa at 17. She was enrolled at a local community college but dropped out before the second semester. Jalen nodded slowly. That must've been when she got pregnant. Yes, Dr. Gates said. Records indicate she resided in a shared apartment in Northeast D.C. The hospital noted she came in alone. No emergency contact. But she named you Jalen—before she passed. Jalen's hands trembled, but he smiled. She named me? She did, Gates affirmed. Your name was not accidental. Your mom claimed you.

Dr. Gates turned the page. Your father, Kwame Osei, is a prominent entrepreneur in Accra. His portfolio spans fintech and infrastructure. He's well-known in West African business circles. Jalen inhaled. We sent him a letter, along with DNA match confirmation. He has acknowledged you. Silence. He's watching today's taping from Ghana. Jalen blinked. What?

Dr. Gates nodded. He says he's ready to talk. He understands he made a grievous mistake, and that fear kept him from owning what love should've covered. Jalen didn't cry. But the tears were somewhere behind his throat, aching for release. For so long, I believed no one wanted me, he said. She named me, and he saw me.

Gates closed the folder. Jalen, your family tree doesn't begin with shame. It starts with strength, Akua. A woman who taught children under trees, walked through marketplaces in bare feet, and spoke with a bold voice. Who crossed oceans not for escape, but for you.

Jalen finally spoke into the camera. To every kid who doesn't know where they came from, don't accept the idea that you are lost. You are becoming, and sometimes, finding your roots means letting someone else water the soil. After the taping, the producer handed Jalen a small package. Inside was a bracelet, handcrafted in green and gold, with an engraved pendant that read: Akua's Son. Never forgotten. As he left the studio, Carmel and Caleb waited in the car. He walked straight into their arms. No words, just a feeling of belonging, his roots finally unearthed. Hey Carmel, congratulations. She asked, for what? He smiled and said, Pretty in Pink; Gorgeous in Green. She beamed with pride.

LEGACY AND FUTURE

I left Earth to study the future of learning. What I found is this: wisdom is not upward. It is inward. It begins when we return to what matters. – **Ayo**

The early morning light crept through the sheer curtains of the brownstone, landing softly on Ashanti's journal. She sat at her writing desk in her robe, mug of tea cooling beside her, pen poised in mid-air. She had begun the entry days ago: Legacy is not what I leave behind when I die. It's what I offer while I'm still living. But today, the words returned to her with more weight. She reflected on Ayo somewhere above Earth, orbiting the planet inside *Athena IX*, teaching humanity how to learn differently. She could track his vitals, read his status updates, even hear his heartbeat through the shared biosensor watch Caleb had designed. But she missed his voice. His grounding presence. She realized: her legacy wouldn't be a building or a fund or a speech. It would be how her children saw themselves as whole, worthy, and powerful individuals deserving of love. Her pen moved across the page. My legacy is not mine alone and braided through the lives of those I've lifted, and those I've let lift me.

Months after re-entry, Ayo stood on stage at the Uwazi Global Summit, with the Earth behind him projected on a curved screen. He wore no suit, just his flight jacket and the patch of Classroom Alpha. We didn't go to space to escape Earth. We went to bring it with us—to remember that learning isn't about where you are. It's about where you're willing to go. Somewhere, in a classroom in Lagos, a girl opened her tablet and joined the next online lesson. She smiled. She was ready.

Ayo shared that in orbit, everything slows. Inside the dim quiet of the Athena IX Learning Module, I floated, tethered by magnetic soles, gazing out at the Earth through the oval viewport. It was smaller than I imagined. It was not fragile, felt vulnerable, yet powerful. Blue and breathing. He remembered something his father used to say: The world is round, so our steps return to us.

In space, before I fell asleep, I would close my eyes and ask myself the question I had been journaling nightly since liftoff: What is my legacy? I thought of my students at Howard, especially the ones who doubted their place in academia. My experiences will show them they belong. He thought of Uwazi's youth hubs, built from collective dreams and rebellion. He thought of Caleb's music, pulsing with defiance, and Carmie's speeches, woven with clarity and fire. But mostly, he thought of Ashanti, her brilliance, her backbone, her faith that had made all this possible. He rose from a dream and whispered into the silence: Let my legacy be a bridge between people, between possibilities, between Earth and what waits beyond.

Caleb sat on the floor of the innovation hub, laptop on one knee, a soldering tool in his hand, and a speaker prototype glowing beside him. Around him, a group of middle schoolers watched as he tested out a patch of LED cloth that reacted to emotion-tracking sensors. Have you ever thought about what people will remember you for? One of the kids asked out of nowhere. Caleb blinked, caught off guard. Then he smirked. Yeah. I used to think it'd be that kid who never followed the rules. The kids laughed. But now? He continued, I want people to remember me as the one who made tech feel like a heartbeat. He paused. Legacy isn't about being famous. It's about making someone braver because you showed them a way forward.

In the quiet of her room, Carmel packed her last suitcase. Her passport sat neatly beside a well-worn leather journal. On the inside cover, Ashanti had written: Write as if the future is listening. Carmel paused, holding the book to her chest. She thought of the young girls she'd be working with in Accra—students navigating justice systems and schools, dreams and disappointments. She didn't want to save them. She tried to listen to them. To learn with them. She realized that her role wasn't to be the voice in the room, but to make room for other voices. She wrote in the journal: Legacy is the echo of your presence in places you never stood. I want to build echoes that carry truth, tenderness, and courage.

ECHOES IN ACCRA

As the plane descended, Jalen gently pressed his forehead against the window. Below, the red clay roads and lush palms sprawled like veins reaching toward the heart of something ancient and waiting. His hands trembled, not from fear, but from something more sacred. He was going home. A place he had never seen. A mother he never knew, and a name he now carried with reverence: Akua's son.

As the aircraft doors opened and the warm West African sun bathed the tarmac, Carmel stepped off first, followed by Zen Chan, Uwazi's Chief Engagement Officer. Jalen hesitated at the door. The air in Accra held the scent of mango, motor oil, and sea breeze. With one deep breath, he stepped into the light. The welcome was thunderous. About 250 people had gathered.

Some wore traditional kente cloth. Others held banners that read:
Akua's Son Comes Home—Kwame's Heir.

Drums beat from a nearby courtyard. Women ululated with pride. Men clapped and embraced. Jalen's eyes widened as a woman with high cheekbones and soft eyes rushed forward, Akua's sister, his aunt, Ama. You look just like her, she said, cupping his face. I've waited my whole life to hear that, Jalen whispered. Then came his father.

Kwame Osei, tall, solemn, dressed in a white agbada embroidered with gold thread. He didn't speak right away. He simply fell to one knee, arms open, a tear tracking down his weathered face. I failed your mother, he said, but I will not fail you. The crowd murmured, some weeping. Others clapped. A few were kneeling in reverence. In this land, reunion was holy. Jalen pulled his father up. We can't rewrite the beginning, he said. "But we can honor her with what we write next.

Carmel stood just outside the swell of the crowd, notebook in hand. She had come not just as Jalen's sister in spirit, but to serve Uwazi's Girls for Justice project, supporting adolescent girls as they navigate the education and justice systems. She wasn't there to lead. She was there to listen.

Earlier that morning, Zen had reminded her gently: Your power is in your presence, not your performance. Now, standing in a sun-dappled school courtyard just outside Jamestown, Carmel watched as girls debated, laughed, cried, and resisted being erased by poverty and patriarchy. You're from America, one girl said. Are you here to save us from the tyranny and the exploitation of colonization? Carmel knelt beside her. No. I'm here to walk with you. To learn what it means to be resilient.

Later, in her journal, she wrote:

> Legacy is the echo of your presence in places you never stood.
> I want to build echoes that carry truth, tenderness, and courage.

That evening, Jalen and his family went to the compound for an official naming ceremony. An ancestral stool was given to him to sit upon, as incense burned. Drummers played low rhythms as village elders poured libations to honor Akua's spirit.

When the moment came, Ama rose and announced:

> We name him Kojo Akua-Jalen Osei. He is his mother's song and his father's return. He is a bridge between yesterday and tomorrow.

The crowd chanted: Kojo Akua-Jalen Osei!

Jalen closed his eyes and let the name settle on him like a garment long overdue.

Zen watched it all with quiet reverence. As Uwazi's Chief Engagement Officer, he had led launches on four continents. But this-this was not about strategy. The emphasis of this launch would be on belonging. He leaned over to Carmel. Do you feel that? Yeah, she whispered. It's the sound of a story healing.

Under a sky bursting with stars, Jalen walked through the compound in silence. He touched the mud walls of the home his mother once visited. He sat beside a mango tree planted the year she left Ghana. He whispered to himself: 'I am not alone. I was lost, but now I am found, and I have become planted.'

On the flight back to Washington, Carmel reopened her journal. She wrote one final line before falling asleep on Zen's shoulder: Sometimes, coming home isn't about finding a place; it's about finding the people who were waiting for your echo to return.

UNAPOLOGETICALLY CARMEL — JUNIOR YEAR AT HOWARD

Carmel MWendo-Joseph had learned to tiptoe through the world. She was not shy, definitely not invisible, but moved with intentionality. This way of being came from observing Ashanti, her mom. She walked the sunlit pathways of Howard University's campus with a rhythm all her own, with a bit of part poetry and algorithm. Students waved at her, professors knew her name, and alumni called her a rising star. But inside, Carmel still felt like the high school girl who sat in the back row, letting others shine. She hadn't changed. But the world around her had.

When Carmel enrolled at Howard at sixteen, no one knew she had earned nearly thirty college credits during her high school years. She had quietly applied herself to advanced placement, dual enrollment, and independent learning programs while balancing her family's whirlwind of innovation, Uwazi projects, and spiritual transformation. By the time she arrived at Howard, Carmel was officially classified as a second-semester sophomore. But she told no one. Not because she wanted to deceive them. But because she didn't think it was important. She wanted to be a Howard student and enjoy her journey. The moment Carmel's accelerated status was revealed was dramatic and accidental. It was during a planning meeting with her Alpha Kappa Alpha Sorority, Inc. chapter, Pretty in Pink, Gorgeous in Green, where the sisters were preparing for a regional leadership retreat.

The chapter advisor, Ms. Laila Simmons, had been reviewing academic records to confirm eligibility for leadership nominations. She looked up, brow furrowed. Carmel, can you come here for a second? Carmel blinked, confused. Yes, ma'am? You are listed officially as a junior, not a sophomore. Why didn't you say anything? A hush fell over the room. One of the sisters whispered, Wait, what? Another said, She's been on campus less than two years! Carmel smiled nervously. I guess I didn't think it was that important. The room burst into reactions: shock, admiration, a tinge of envy. But then one of her line sisters, Imani, leaned forward and said softly. You don't need to explain, sis. You walk in excellence, and we see you. We're proud of you. Carmel exhaled, for the first time that week, she smiled without hesitation.

It wasn't just her academic status that set her apart. Her work with Uwazi, especially her leadership on the *Harmonic Code* project for neurodiverse children, had earned her features in student newspapers, tech newsletters, and even a spotlight as an HBCU Innovator to Watch. To others, she was the dream student: brilliant, gracious, mission-driven. But for Carmel, attention felt like a distortion. In high school, she was quiet, often overlooked, and completely comfortable in the shadows. Popularity was never a goal; it was an accident of impact. She sometimes wished she could rewind to simpler days. But deep down, she knew her discomfort was a sign of growth in disguise.

One evening, after a long day of classes and sorority meetings, Carmel stood before her mirror in her dorm room, still wearing her pink and green blazer. She studied her reflection, not the outfit, but the woman. She whispered: You are not the noise. You are the note in the crescendo and diminuendo. Then she opened her journal and wrote, I didn't come here to impress. I came to serve, listen, lead when necessary, and follow when it matters. Let them be surprised. I'd rather be authentic than understood.

Later that week, the AKA chapter voted Carmel in as Program Chair for the upcoming semester. When she tried to decline, Imani nudged her. Sis, this isn't about being perfect. It's about being present. Your presence already inspires us; now you get to organize the path. She created programming that blended community tech labs, healing circles, and career mentorship for teen girls. She still sat in the back sometimes, listening, learning. Now, when she spoke, others leaned in. Not because she was loud. But because she had something to say.

At the end of that semester, Carmel walked across the Yard alone, the air crisp with fall. She paused under the Frederick Douglass statue, looked around at the legacy she was part of, and smiled. This is who I am, she thought. Not a prodigy. Not a headline. Just a girl walking faithfully in the purpose written before her, with quiet resolve, she whispered, I belong here.

CALEB GOES TO COLLEGE

Caleb MWendo-Joseph was a conundrum to most. Brilliant, sarcastic yet deeply intuitive, grounded in logic but pulled by wonder. He didn't dislike school. He just didn't trust the system to recognize the kind of intelligence he carried: the kind that wrote code like jazz and questioned everything from gravity to grace.

After finishing high school, he watched from the sidelines as his sister, Carmel, soared through Howard University like a constellation—Alpha Kappa Alpha, Uwazi leadership, junior year status, before she turned eighteen. His father, Dr. Ayo Joseph, had recently begun serving as a tenured professor in STEM education at Howard, where he combined his passion for space exploration with his commitment to student development. His mother, Ashanti, was a keynote speaker, board chair, and global thought leader across the technology industry. Caleb was home, spending most of his time coding and thinking. Observing from a quiet corner of the world, where nothing was required but everything was possible, he was a free spirit.

It was a Sunday afternoon when Jalen showed up. No grand entry, just his usual smile, a hoodie, and his signature phrase: Yo. Are you good? Caleb nodded from the couch, fingers dancing across a keyboard. Jalen watched him work, mesmerized by the effortless logic and artistry happening on the screen. After a few minutes, he sat beside Caleb, exhaled, and began gently. You know. You're the most intelligent person I've ever met. Caleb chuckled, still focused. You need to meet more people. Nah, I'm serious. I've been around. I spent time in group homes, on the streets, at the church, and Howard. Nobody I know thinks like you. Caleb paused, sensing the shift.

I'm not saying college is the only path, Jalen added. But man, not going at all? That's not rebellion, that's retreat and hiding. You've got gifts, and you're letting them sit in draft mode. Silence. Then Jalen leaned in closer. You have what I didn't. A foundation. Parents who believe in you. A sister who admires you. A room full of love. If none of that gets to you, this should: I'd be proud of you, bro. Like really proud. Caleb blinked, emotion quietly rising. Giving up this opportunity is a waste of your talent. Honestly, it breaks my heart.

Caleb sighed. Fine, okay. You win. Jalen perked up. Wait, what? I'll register. I'll go to Howard. Are you happy now? Jalen jumped to his feet, fist-pumping the air. That's what I'm talking about, baby! Let's go!" Caleb rolled his eyes but couldn't stop the smile forming on his lips.

Later that week, he went online to register for Howard admissions. His transcripts were impeccable. His test scores were near perfect. But his essay? Barely 250 words. I wasn't sure I wanted to be here. But here I am. Maybe that's enough to start. The counselor blinked at the brevity. Then she looked at the name on the file. Wait, are you Dr. Joseph's son and Carmel's brother? Caleb sighed. Yeah. That's me. She smiled. Welcome to the family.

After registration, Caleb got on the train alone and visited the Howard University campus, walking the Yard alone. It was a familiar space. He spent time here with his friend Jalen. There were times he commuted to campus with his Dad and sister. He passed the technology building where Ayo lectured. He passed the library where Carmel was probably leading a study circle or organizing a speaker series. He saw students laughing under trees, others playing chess in the quad. A couple argued over the most influential rapper at a vending machine. It was a strange, chaotic harmony. For the first time in a long while, he didn't feel like an outsider. He felt like a node in a living network system—a small, significant signal in the network of Black excellence.

Back home, Carmel screamed when she saw the Howard hoodie in Caleb's bag. No. You didn't. You registered? Caleb nodded, then smirked. Yeah, yeah. Don't make it weird. Ashanti pulled him into a long, quiet hug. Ayo just clapped a hand on his back and whispered: This doesn't make us proud. You already made us proud. Taking this step just helps you realize it for yourself. Jalen sat at the kitchen counter, arms crossed, beaming like a proud big brother. Told you, genius.

That night, Caleb opened a new file on his tablet. He titled it: Code of Belonging. He first sketched a tree with roots and various fruits bearing on the branches. He began typing: I am here. Not because I need to prove anything. But because my presence is a form of resistance, my success is a form of inheritance. I am a MWendo-Joseph, and this is one step in the family's legacy.

Caleb had never been one for crowds, study groups, or school spirit. But there he was—backpack slung over one shoulder, navigating the buzz of Howard University's first-week energy like a reluctant Black panther probing the environment. It wasn't the classes that intimidated him. He'd devoured quantum mechanics textbooks for fun and coded his own neural net language model at sixteen. No, it was everything else—the noise, the cultural codes, the unspoken rhythms of HBCU life. He spent many years in the Old Pueblo, experiencing limited diversity in his life, outside of his immediate family.

People greeted him like they already knew him. The AKA's knew who he was and would approach him with, You're Carmel's brother, right? People would ask what it was like being involved with Uwazi. He wasn't used to being known before being seen. In the classroom, Caleb excelled, but not because he aimed to impress. His curiosity was endless. He challenged his professors respectfully but relentlessly. In Computer Science 204, when the instructor introduced blockchain theory, Caleb raised his hand

and asked: How are we building systems of trust when they're still designed by those who profit from mistrust? There was a pause, some people nodded, then scribbled notes. The professor responded:

The premise of your question is spot on. Many of our current systems, particularly in areas such as social media, finance, and specific aspects of information dissemination, are designed with business models that can inadvertently (or sometimes directly) benefit from mistrust. For instance:

- Social media algorithms often thrive on engagement driven by sensationalism, outrage, or division, which erodes trust in information and one another.
- Financial systems can be opaque, benefiting intermediaries who profit from complex transactions rather than transparent, direct dealings.
- Data collection practices frequently maximize profit from selling personal information, leading to distrust in how our data is handled and used.

When the primary incentive for designers and corporations is maximizing profit, and that profit can be increased by a lack of transparency, exploiting biases, or fostering dependence, building genuine trust becomes incredibly difficult.

Caleb responded: Ultimately, building truly trustworthy systems in a world where profit motives often conflict with those goals is a continuous struggle, not a destination. It requires:

- Constant vigilance and advocacy from users, regulators, and ethical designers.
- Innovation in technologies that inherently bake in transparency and decentralization.
- A shift in corporate culture that recognizes the long-term value of trust over short-term financial gains.

It's a dynamic interplay between those who seek to profit, those who demand transparency and trust, and the evolving technological landscape.

Caleb didn't just code; he questioned code and spoke it into existence, asking its ethics, implications, and why.

But beyond the classroom, Caleb felt like a beta version of himself, still debugging. He struggled with small talk. When students gathered for social mixers or homecoming prep, he often opted out. He preferred the lab, his dorm, or quiet coffee runs.

Until Professor Mensah, one of Ayo's colleagues, stopped him after class. You have a gift, Mr. MWendo-Joseph. But even the brightest signal needs a network. Caleb nodded, not ready to reply. But the words stayed with him. That evening, he logged into the university's community platform and signed up for three new groups:

- Code for Justice Initiative
- Black Male Alliance
- Uwazi Campus Corps

It was the Uwazi Campus Corps that shifted everything. Run by students and mentored by Uwazi leaders, the corps worked on real-world community tech projects—from AI-powered learning tools in under-resourced schools to digital mental health platforms for urban teens. In the first meeting, Caleb mostly observed. But when the conversation turned to designing an accessibility app for visually impaired users, he couldn't stay silent. What if we flip the UX logic entirely? Treat auditory experience as the design lead, not the afterthought? There was quiet in the room.

Caleb began meeting weekly with Professor Mensah and occasionally joined Ayo's guest lectures—not as his son, but as a contributor. He found a quiet rhythm with Jalen, who remained his grounding force. So you still think college is a scam? Jalen teased one afternoon. Not entirely, Caleb replied. It's more useful when you ignore the hype and build your blueprint. That's real, Jalen smiled. But don't forget to enjoy it, too. You get to live your brilliance out loud now.

One day in October, Carmel pulled Caleb aside during a break in their overlapping seminar. When will you be speaking at one of our leadership panels? Why would I do that?" Caleb asked, surprised. Because your story matters, she said. Other quiet geniuses are walking these halls. Maybe they need to hear that it's okay not to fit the mold. He didn't answer right away. But that night, he drafted a speech.

By semester's end, Caleb had submitted his first academic paper to a peer-reviewed journal, helped develop a beta version of the accessibility app, and most surprisingly, volunteered to co-lead a campus forum on Black tech ethics. During Howard's midwinter chapel, when the guest speaker mentioned *the courage of silence in a world addicted to noise*, Caleb leaned forward and smiled. Back in his room, he opened his tablet. He drew an image with the caption, Wisdom grows in community.

DORM LIFE – NEW SPACES, NEW SOULS

Carmel and Caleb had never imagined they'd be living on campus, especially not at the same time. At home in Kalorama, their home was filled with an abundance of love, space, and smart appliances that could practically do their homework. But it lacked one thing: After a conversation with Ashanti that ended with her trademark line, 'You don't grow muscle where there's no resistance,' Carmel announced she was applying for on-campus housing. You'll miss your closet in exactly two hours, Caleb teased. Maybe. But I'll find myself in the next two. He didn't admit it then, but her words stuck. When Jalen brought it up again, casually over burritos one night. Imagine being late-night coders and roomies, bro, Caleb paused. Two weeks later, their housing applications were submitted. They were moving out. Not because anything was wrong at home, but because everything had matured. It was time.

Carmel's roommate assignment was with Imani Carter, her line sister in Alpha Kappa Alpha and a natural-born event planner with a dazzling smile and a color-coded calendar. Are you ready for late-night talks, face masks, and spreadsheets? Imani teased as they unpacked. I was born ready, Carmel grinned, hanging a pink and green banner that read: Sisterhood is Service with Style.

Their dorm room quickly became a soft haven of scented candles, throw pillows, and coordinated study sessions. But it was also a think tank. An incubator of ideas for sorority programs, service campaigns, and girlhood dreams turned into legacy plans. One night, as they were scrolling through upcoming chapter events, Imani looked at Carmel and said: You don't just belong here. You lead here even when you're quiet. Carmel felt a surge of gratitude.

Meanwhile, Caleb's dorm room had a slightly different vibe. Less rose gold, more LED lights—fewer playlists, more debugging. Jalen moved in as if he were returning to a tribe. He brought a duffle bag, a box of theology books, two jars of shea butter, and shared a mission: to build brilliance and laugh often. We're like Wakanda meets Silicon Valley, Jalen declared, placing a poster of Malcolm X and a Raspberry Pi kit on their desk. Caleb grunted more like Tech Bros with a Bible. Hey, balance is key, Jalen shot back. Jesus and JavaScript. Their nights were a mash-up of code sprints, gospel hip hop, and debates about everything from the ethics of AI to the meaning of grace. Despite their different starting points, their dorm became more than a shared room—it became a space of healing, imagination, and brotherhood.

The twins didn't see each other every day now, but when they did, it was sweet chaos. A quick dinner at the student center. A late-night chat on the quad. Jalen is teasing Carmel about her new love for K-drama. Imani is borrowing Caleb's extra charger while calling him the honorary soror tech guy. There were even Sundays where all four would grab brunch, hash out ideas for a Table Church service, or brainstorm a Uwazi youth app while laughing over waffles.

Ashanti and Ayo visited one weekend, watching from the sidelines as their children buzzed in complete autonomy. They've found their wings, Ayo said, arms crossed proudly, and their tribe, Ashanti whispered, eyes misty.

EMPTY SPACES

The Kalorama brownstone once danced with youthful energy. Now, in the quiet, every creaking stair and echoing hallway told the same story: the twins left the nest. Carmel and Caleb had moved into Howard dorms, a milestone the family knew would come one day, just not one they'd emotionally prepared for. Their rooms were still tidy, their books still stacked, but the music, the late-night debates, the open refrigerator doors, and the random hallway hugs were missing. Even Uno and Duos, their spirited rescue pups, felt it. Uno stood by Carmel's closed door each morning, tail twitching, head tilted, waiting. Duos had taken to dragging Caleb's old hoodie out of the laundry hamper just to lie on it. Without their human companions sneaking them treats and belly rubs between Zoom classes and coding sessions, the house felt empty.

Ashanti was the first to name the feeling. One evening, while pouring tea and watching Uno paw at the glass patio door, she whispered: This house feels too big without their voices and activities. Ayo looked up from his laptop, glasses sliding down his nose. We raised them to fly," he said. Now I just want them to circle back home and then. She smiled gently, her eyes soft with memory. They will. But in the meantime, I miss their presence. It was a truth both understood. So, instead of stewing in the quiet, Ashanti called Alma and Agustin. Come for dinner, she said. Bring Bruno. Let's fill this space with life again.

Alma arrived with her signature saffron rice and a watercolor sketchbook tucked under her arm. Agustin brought fresh Cuban bread and a bottle of red wine. Bruno bounded through the front door, tail wagging wildly, launching himself straight into Uno and Duos' joyful chaos. The table, once set for four, now hosted laughter and rich conversation. Ashanti and Alma soon found themselves seated by the kitchen window, sipping tea as the golden hour cast warmth over their faces. Have you given more thought to your dream?" Ashanti asked.

Alma hesitated, then nodded. Yes. She dreamed of one day opening a nonprofit that would give families not just homes, but dignity. She wanted to show young Latina women they could rise with passion and dreams. I also want to open a studio-gallery space, a place where art, storytelling, and healing can live together—a sanctuary for those who don't see themselves in traditional museums.

Ashanti's eyes lit up. Then we build it. Let's blueprint it over lunch this week. Meanwhile, in the den, Ayo and Agustin were watching a Nationals game, each with a beer in hand, trading stories from their youth. Have you ever thought about coaching Little League?" Agustin asked. There was no fanfare, just connection—like brothers finding rhythm in a shared silence.

Coach Melody began stopping by more often. She, too, had felt the pang of transition as the kids moved out, the business expanded, and the shift from doing to guiding took hold. Her coaching business was thriving, and she had recently begun onboarding a cohort of global coaches, including voices from Brazil, Kenya, India, and the American South, all trained in her method of spiritually informed leadership. I want to build a coaching fellowship, she shared with Ashanti. One that centers divine leadership in diverse tongues. Ashanti lit up. Let's co-host a retreat. Right here. D.C. needs this. The idea planted itself like a seed in spring soil.

Week by week, the once-silent brownstone started buzzing again, not with teenage chatter, but with something just as alive: *new purpose.* Ashanti began mentoring young women CEOs through a new initiative linked to Uwazi. Ayo took on a side project, developing an AI curriculum for community schools.
Uno and Duos, satisfied with regular playdates with Bruno, seemed to bark less at the mail carrier. They were still parents, just to a bigger family now—mentors, elders, architects of a legacy far beyond biology.

One night, after Alma and Agustin had gone home and the dishwasher hummed in the background, Ayo pulled Ashanti into a quiet dance in the living room. We're not empty, he said, swaying gently. We're just expanding into a new season of life. Ashanti rested her head on his shoulder. Empty spaces are just rooms waiting for new stories. So, they danced in their quiet house, feet bare, hearts full, writing the next chapter with every step.

COMING HOME
WITH NEWS

It had been nearly two months since Carmel and Caleb had last walked through the doors of the Kalorama brownstone. In truth, it wasn't far, just a short train ride from Howard, but time had shifted. The twins were navigating independence, identity, and an exhilarating world of academia and friendship. Their absence had created both silence and space at home, but now, with one weekend planned and carefully plotted, the space in the house would once again be filled.

Uno and Duos sensed it first. The tails wagged. The scratching at the door began. And when the train finally arrived, the dogs exploded into the type of joy only a pet reunion can offer. I missed you, too, Carmel laughed, bending to let Duos nearly knock her over. Okay, okay—let them breathe!" Caleb grinned, trying to wrangle Uno, who had a new trick: full-body hugs.

Right behind them came Jalen, now more than just Caleb's roommate—he was family, as comfortable in the brownstone as he was in church or code. And then there was Imani, Carmel's roommate and line sister, holding a small tote bag and a pie wrapped in foil. Hi, Mrs. Joseph, Imani greeted, offering the pie with a proud smile. Oh, please, Ashanti beamed. Call me Ashanti. We don't do formal things when there's sweet potato pie involved.

The weekend visit unfolded like a long exhale—meals stretching into laughter, soft music floating through the kitchen, and Coach Melody arriving just in time for Friday night tea and talk. You kids have grown, she said, looking around the table. Tell me about it, Ayo muttered. They don't call, don't write. We text! Caleb argued, mock-defensive. Memes are not communication, Ashanti quipped, passing around plates. As if on cue, the doorbell rang. It was Alma, Augustin, and Bruno who pounced inside. Uno and Duos resumed their joyful chaos, the house filled with fur and family.

It was Saturday night when the conversation shifted. Everyone had gathered in the living room—pillows on the floor, plates balanced on knees, laughter from the kitchen still echoing. Ashanti looked at her children. You two look like you're hiding something. Carmel exchanged glances with Caleb. Then with Imani. Caleb sighed. Jalen raised an eyebrow. Should we tell them? Carmel whispered. Now or never, Caleb shrugged. Ayo leaned forward. Tell us what? There was a beat of silence. We're launching a new student startup, Carmel said. Focused on AI-powered educational equity tools, Caleb added. Imani jumped in: We're working with Howard's Innovation Hub. It'll be student-led, faculty-supported, and funded partially by Uwazi.

Ashanti blinked. Wait a minute, you're building a company? A project. For now, Jalen offered. But we think it could grow into something more. We call it EchoED, Carmel explained. Echo, as in the legacy of sound, amplifies student voices. Caleb jumped in and expanded that Echo is an actual computer syntax to send text to a display. ED for education. It's rooted in what we've learned at Howard and what Uwazi has taught us. Coach Melody placed her mug slowly. Her face glowed. Legacy work in the making.

The rest of the evening dissolved into brainstorming, questions, story-sharing, and vision. Alma shared thoughts on cultural integration. Agustin offered to introduce them to tech contacts from his early career in Mexico. Ayo listened with pride in his eyes, mainly staying quiet, while Ashanti scribbled ideas into her journal, occasionally asking," Have you thought about community licensing"?

At one point, Carmel and Imani stepped outside onto the patio. They're not mad, are they? Imani asked. Mad? Carmel grinned. They're already planning the second phase. Back inside, Caleb nudged Jalen. Thanks for pushing me, bro. If you hadn't, encourage me. Nah, Jalen said softly. You always had it. I just turned up the volume.

That night, long after everyone went to bed, Ayo and Ashanti stood at the staircase, looking out over the now-quiet living room. They're not our babies anymore, Ashanti whispered. No, Ayo replied. They're builders now of tools, communities, and futures.

In that whole house, once defined by its quiet, now transformed by purpose, every room pulsed again with life, vision, and the steady rhythm of becoming.

THE FAMILY COMMITS
TO KINGDOM LIVING

The sanctuary of The Table church was warm with expectancy, not from incense or rituals, but from the collective breath of people yearning for something more: truth, grace, renewal. The Joseph family had made The Table their spiritual home. What began as an invitation from Jalen had become a rhythm of Sunday mornings, quiet prayers, and bold questions. Ayo and Ashanti sat side by side, hands interlocked. Carmel was radiant, her face beaming with anticipation. Caleb was there, too. Very quiet, observant, and skeptical, but present. Jalen sat at the end of the row, shoulders relaxed, but soul stirred. He belonged here, not just in the pew, but in the Joseph family. Ayo had become a second father, offering wisdom, challenge, and most importantly, *presence*.

That morning, Pastor Mavis Anokye stood at the pulpit with a gentle authority. Today, she said, we baptize those who have declared their commitment to Kingdom Living, living by the spirit of justice, mercy, humility, and love. Today, brave souls step into sacred water. The baptismal pool at the front glistened under soft lights. Ayo went first. A proud Black man, educator-astronaut, scholar, and now, a disciple walking deeper into faith. As he emerged from the water, he looked toward Ashanti and smiled with quiet reverence. Then Ashanti, graceful and resolute, had led many through complex boardrooms and global initiatives. But this was something else. This experience was personal. Carmel followed, her joy effervescent. She nearly skipped into the pool. Are you sure you're ready? Pastor Mavis asked with a grin. Born ready, Carmel replied. Then she was immersed. When she rose, she whispered, I belong, with tears running down her cheek.

Pastor Mavis looked at the clipboard. That concludes our—A voice from the back called out: Wait, there's one more! Heads turned. People stood. Eyes squinted toward the aisle. From behind the curtain, a figure emerged slowly. Slim. Slightly unsure. He walked toward the baptismal pool as if drawn by something beyond himself. Gasps. Whispers. Then silence.

One of the men's leaders stepped beside the pool and asked: Do you freely accept Jesus as your Savior? He looked around. The room disappeared. His family faded into a peripheral blur. He thought of his grandfather, the one who used to sing hymns while tinkering with old tools in the garage. Then he said: Yes. I do. The water embraced him, and time paused. When he came up, gasping for breath, he felt it. A surge and pull blended with stillness and electricity all at once. Above him, soaring gently just under the rafters, a white dove. He gasped again, not from water, but from *wonder*. Jalen's mouth dropped open. What?! What is happening right now?! Ayo stood up. Ashanti covered her mouth with her hand. Carmel was frozen, tears already forming. I saw it, he whispered to himself. I saw it!

Jalen sprinted to the baptismal pool and grabbed Caleb in a massive hug. What! What! When did you decide this?! Caleb was shaking, half-laughing, half-crying. I don't know, man! I felt my grandpa's hand tapping me on the shoulder. I heard his voice say, It's okay. Go on. Carmel ran in next, wrapping them both in a joyful tangle of tears and laughter. Ashanti joined them, then Ayo. The seven Kingdom Living principles are alive, Ashanti said. Certainly is, Ayo replied, his voice catching as he pulled Caleb into a strong, proud hug. The sanctuary erupted in praise. Not noisy. Not forced. But sacred. The choir sang:

> I hear you calling from Heaven
>
> Calling me by my name
>
> I'm running into your presence
>
> I'll do it again and again
>
> Let me sit at your feet, Lord
>
> Listen to your words
>
> Your peace flows over my life
>
> There's no better place to be

Back home around the dinner table, the house was quieter than usual—each family member deep in reflection. Caleb put down his fork, cleared his throat, and said: I have to share something. Jalen gave him the what-now look. As I came up from the baptism pool, I saw a white dove. Everyone looked up. What did you say? Jalen asked again, this time seriously. I saw a white dove flying above me just after I emerged from the water. You saw the Holy Spirit? Carmel asked softly. Caleb shrugged, nervous but confident. I don't know if it was a hallucination or adrenaline or some light trick, but that's what I saw. Ayo put his hand over his heart. That's real, son. Ashanti smiled at Caleb with tears in her eyes. You've always had the mind of a skeptic. But maybe now you're also growing the heart of a believer.

That night, Caleb opened his tablet and began sketching the experience. He wrote just one line: I don't need to know everything to say yes to something real. Then he wrote another: I saw the dove. And the dove saw me.

THE TABLE EXTENDED BEYOND WALLS

It began with a pot of soup and an uncomfortable question. Why are our tables only full on Sunday? The question came from Pastor Mavis one evening during a post-service meal. Several church members gathered at the Josephs' house with Jalen and a few other members of The Table. Laughter, gospel jazz, and the scent of collard greens filled the air, but the room quieted when she spoke. We preach community. We worship in love. But how many of us are serving the people right outside our doors? Ayo leaned forward, thoughtful. You mean providing meals to the homeless programs? Feeding is part of it, she said. But people need dignity more than bread. What if The Table became more than a place to gather? What if it became a launchpad for reclaimed dignity and possibilities?

Over the next few weeks, ideas began to swirl and shape. Car-mel, inspired by her work in Ghana, compiled a list of initiatives that uplifted youth voices, centered on healing justice, and lever-aged technology for community empowerment. Jalen suggested partnerships with D.C. organizations to provide mentorship for youth who had aged out of foster care, like he once did. Ashanti offered to host workshops for women entrepreneurs of color, sharing her leadership experience and mentorship tools. Ayo dreamed of a Saturday School that blended STEM and story-telling, so children saw themselves not only as coders, but as keepers of culture. Caleb, quiet but present, began prototyping an app called Extend the Table, a mobile platform that con-nects volunteers, resources, and opportunities for service across wards.

Their first community event was on a warm Saturday in the heart of Ward 7. They called it: The Table Beyond Walls: Love. Learning. Liberation. Dozens gathered in an open field, where folding chairs formed circles of dialogue, and food trucks served jerk tofu alongside fried catfish. Under a tent, Carmel led a storytelling circle for teenage girls navigating the justice sys-tem. Your voice is valid, she said. Even when the world forgets to listen. Across the park, Jalen laughed as he helped a young man fix a broken bicycle chain, sharing stories of resilience between grease-stained hands. Ashanti stood beneath a canopy marked SHEbuilds, talking to women about access to capital, grant writ-ing, and boardroom confidence. Caleb stood at the tech booth, showing local organizers how to use the Extend the Table app. He didn't say much, but his code spoke volumes.

In the afternoon, Ayo gathered a group of children near a small whiteboard and a telescope. Today, you will see how science meets story, he said. You know how far the stars are? Yet, you can still see them. He paused. That means distance doesn't make something less real. Just because you come from a hard place doesn't mean you aren't able to achieve greatness. A little girl raised her hand. What was it like going to space? Going to space was scary, he smiled. Although I trained to feel weightless, I was unable to stop myself from bumping into things. The room burst into laughter.

What began as a one-day event evolved into a movement.

- Monthly Table Beyond Walls gatherings sprouted across the city.
- Carmel launched a youth arts and justice fellowship.
- Caleb's app reached over 500 users in its first quarter.
- Ayo and Ashanti started a podcast called *"Kingdom & Culture,"* highlighting stories of faith in action.
- Jalen became the official coordinator of *Brothers' Table*, a mentorship circle for young men navigating foster care, grief, and transition.

Every month, Pastor Mavis opened the gathering with the exact words: The call is not to fix people. The call is to *see* them. Seeing is the beginning of every miracle.

One evening, after a long day of community organizing, the Josephs and Jalen sat around their kitchen table. Ashanti looked at the crew, smiling but exhausted, joyful but weathered. This is Kingdom Living. Carmel raised her glass to tables with no walls. Caleb tapped his fingers against his glass and added, to code that makes compassion scalable. Jalen chuckled, to doves. I'm still not over Caleb seeing that dove. Laughter broke through the room like a sunrise. In her journal that night, Carmel wrote: Legacy isn't about being remembered. It's about leaving spaces better than you found them. It's not the chairs we sit in but the arms we open that matter. The Table was never just about Sunday. The intention was for everyday use.

REFERENCES

Megan Dailey Higgs. 2023. The soup we are cooked in.
Retrieved from: https://critical-inference.com/the-soup-we-are-cooked-in/
#:~:text=The%20soup%20metaphor%20conveys%20som
ething,now%20just%20feels%20like%20us.

EPILOGUE

The Kalorama brownstone, once filled with the gentle hum of a family finding its place, now thrived with a richer, more settled tone. It was a late autumn evening, the kind where the air carried the sharp scent of fallen leaves and the promise of longer nights. Inside, the MWendo-Joseph home shone again, not just with soft lamplight but with the warmth of shared victories and quiet understanding.

Ayo, back on Earth for a year now, still carried the stillness of space in his eyes, but his laughter was fuller and more grounded. He sat on the living room sofa, a well-worn copy of his published paper, Distributed Belonging: Learning Across Gravity, open on his lap. He was no longer just an educator; he was a bridge builder, with his new course at Howard, Learning Beyond Borders, a testament to his expanded vision. Uno and Duos, older now and even more prone to naps, snored contentedly at his feet, their gentle rhythm a familiar comfort.

Ashanti moved through the kitchen, preparing hibiscus tea, her movements smooth and unhurried. The past year, with its deep-fake attacks and Kathy's passing, had tested her in ways she hadn't imagined. But she had emerged not only intact but also transformed. Her leadership at Uwazi now emphasizes radical transparency, local ownership, story-first development, and co-creation over consumption."The crisis hadn't broken her; it had refined her, anchoring her leadership in vulnerability and faith. She was learning that healing had a rhythm, and she was choosing what came next.

Upstairs, the twins' rooms, once empty spaces, now reflected vibrant signs of their thriving lives. Carmel was home from Howard for the break, her journal open on her desk. Her Pretty in Pink, Gorgeous in Green aspirations had blossomed into a fierce advocacy for digital justice and cultural consent. She was building legal frameworks to protect youth innovations, making room for other voices. Her work in Accra had taught her that legacy is the echo of your presence in places you never stood.

Caleb, now a student at Howard himself, has carved out his unique path. His SoundSkin prototypes have evolved into impactful tools, and he is co-leading the Open Youth IP Collective, making sure young creators keep control of their work. He no longer feels the need to prove himself, knowing that legacy isn't about being famous, it's about making someone braver. His baptism, a quiet moment of deep personal decision, marked a new chapter, confirming that he didn't need to know everything to say yes to something real.

Jalen, now undeniably part of the family, joined them at the dining table, sharing news from his Finding Your Roots journey and the growth of EchoED, the AI-powered educational equity tool he, Carmel, and Caleb were developing. His connection to his Ghanaian roots had strengthened, and he carried his mother's legacy with pride: Akua's Son. Never forgotten.

Later, as the family gathered around the fire pit in the backyard, the cool night air wrapped around them. There was no grand announcement, no dramatic —just the quiet comfort of being together. Ayo looked at Ashanti, their hands meeting in the low light. They had faced the unknown of space and the chaos of the digital world, the sorrow of loss, and the joy of new beginnings. Their dreams had shifted, expanded, and taken on new forms.

Ashanti smiled, resting her head on Ayo's shoulder. What's next for us? she whispered, not out of uncertainty but of endless possibilities. The stars above Kalorama seemed to shimmer in agreement, bearing witness to a legacy still in motion, unfolding, one truth, one dream, one shared heartbeat at a time.

ABOUT THE AUTHOR

Dave A. Cornelius Aka Dr. Dave

As a coach, learning facilitator, and innovator, I collaborate with leaders, individuals, and organizations to develop a vision and plan that advances progress toward success. My coaching practice employs a whole-person coaching ap-  proach that encompasses the Head (Mind), Heart (Spirit), Hands (Action), and Habits (Sustainable Change) to foster profound, lasting transformations in leadership, business, career, and personal growth.

I am a man of faith and believe everyone needs guidance to live a fruitful life. The Holy Spirit is my guiding light. My life has changed since I accepted Christ as my Savior.

I am grateful to everyone I collaborated with, shared with, prayed with, and learned from. Throughout my career, I have developed skills as an innovator, software developer, coach, learning facilitator, author, keynote speaker, community organizer, design thinker, product manager, and lean-agile leader, among others. I am a lifelong learner.

Dr. Dave has authored several books, which are available on Amazon. He is a former member of the Forbes Coaching Council, and his book, "Generative Leadership to Thrive," is featured in the Forbes Executive Council Library. Additionally, he has authored several articles published on Forbes.com.

He created several leadership and team games available on MIRO and GameCrafters.

His podcast and blog, "KnolShare with Dr. Dave," can be found on Spotify, Audible, Apple Podcasts, and www.KnolShare.org.

ASHANTI MWENDO

The Ashanti MWendo series is a fiction story about an amazing Black woman leading a technology company. The series includes:
(1) The Innovation Catalyst, Leading with Empathy.
(2) Beyond The Windowsill.

In The Innovation Catalyst, Leading with Empathy, we follow the inspiring journey of Ashanti MWendo as she takes on her new role as Chief Product Officer at Avante Garde Virtual Reality. Amidst a world of mediocre customer sentiment and outdated technology platforms, Ashanti must confront the challenge of revitalizing the company's once-popular fantasy vacation VR product, which has been plagued by motion sickness issues.

In the sequel of the Ashanti MWendo series, Beyond The Windowsill, we embark on a captivating journey with Ashanti as she navigates the complexities of leading two tech giants, Avant-Garde Metaverse (AGM) and Uwazi while balancing the demands of motherhood and partnership. The tapestry of Ashanti's life is richly woven with diverse threads, each essential to her life's journey. Her husband, Ayo, and twin 12-year-old children, Carmel and Caleb, who live on the spectrum with exceptional gifts, provide her with a steadfast anchor of love and support.

The Innovation Catalyst, Leading With Empathy (Ashanti Mwendo Book 1)

We follow the inspiring journey of Ashanti MWendo as she takes on her new role as Chief Product Officer at Avante Garde Virtual

Reality. Amidst a world of mediocre customer sentiment and outdated technology platforms, Ashanti must confront the challenge of revitalizing the company's once-popular fantasy vacation VR product, which has been plagued by motion sickness issues.

As the metaverse revolution looms on the horizon, Ashanti's determination and leadership are put to the test. With the company's future at stake, she embarks on an ambitious quest to transform the underperforming VR product and nurture a culture of innovation within Avante Garde. By championing an entrepreneurship program for internal employees and community partners, Ashanti seeks to unleash the untapped potential of her team.

Ashanti's journey is a gripping tale of perseverance and triumph in the face of adversity. Through Ashanti's visionary leadership, we explore the importance of embracing change, fostering creativity, and empowering individuals to make a lasting impact on the ever-evolving metaverse world of virtual reality. This powerful narrative serves as a reminder that when faced with seemingly insurmountable obstacles, the human spirit is capable of achieving extraordinary feats.

Beyond The Windowsill (Ashanti Mwendo Book 2)

In the sequel of the Ashanti MWendo series, we embark on a captivating journey with Ashanti as she navigates the complexities of leading two tech giants, Avant-Garde Metaverse (AGM) and Uwazi, while balancing the demands of motherhood and partnership.

The tapestry of Ashanti's life is richly woven with diverse threads, each essential to her life's journey. Her husband, Ayo, and twin 12-year-old children, Carmel and Caleb, who live on the spectrum with exceptional gifts, provide her with a steadfast anchor of love and support.

As Ashanti spearheads AGM's product development and Uwazi's interim CEO, she must masterfully balance her dual roles, harnessing her agility and vision to spur continuous innovation in both realms. The dynamic world of Uwazi, a nascent venture poised to amplify its Metaverse offerings through the innovative use of AI deepfakes and security tokens, presents Ashanti with new challenges and opportunities.

This captivating sequel will witness Ashanti's unwavering commitment to her family, career, and passion for innovation. We will cheer her on as she overcomes obstacles and achieves new heights, blazing a trail for other women, men, girls, boys, and 'they' to follow.

BOOKS BY THIS AUTHOR

Trust Fidelity: Removing Engagement Friction

Is your team stuck in quicksand? Grinding through the motions but lacking spark?

Introducing Trust Fidelity: Removing Engagement Friction, your blueprint for building a high-performance organization where trust fuels results. Forget forced motivation and hollow engagement surveys. This book explores the hidden force driving productivity and innovation: authentic trust.

Author Dave A. Cornelius, DM, aka Dr. Dave, is a seasoned leadership expert who exposes the invisible friction points hindering your team's potential. Whether it's the dreaded "I wish I could trust them" syndrome or the suffocating grip of micromanagement, Trust Fidelity identifies the culprits and offers practical, actionable strategies to overcome them.

Learn how to:
- Shift from "trust but verify" to "absolutely, always!" and unleash the power of deep-seated trust.
- Break down communication barriers and build bridges of transparency that ignite collaboration.
- Empower your team with ownership and autonomy, fueling creativity and innovation.
- Foster a culture of psychological safety where mistakes are steps toward progress, not stumbling blocks.

Trust Fidelity is your roadmap to ditching the engagement

treadmill and creating a thriving environment where people **don't just work. They believe... Join the trust revolution and watch your team soar to new heights!

Get your copy of Trust Fidelity today and unlock the full potential of your high-performing team.

Generative Leadership To Thrive

The book Generative Leadership to Thrive unfolds as a journey, guiding leaders through a pathway that does not merely seek to navigate through the industrial revolutions and the VUCA environment but also to thrive amidst them. With a harmonious blend of theoretical frameworks, practical strategies, real-world insights, and a human-centered approach, the book establishes a compelling narrative that Generative Leadership, imbued with Ubuntu principles and values and Generative Adaptive Practice (GAP) tenets, is pivotal in crafting a future where organizations, their people, and their customers, do not just survive but markedly thrive.

Generative leadership is a style of leadership that focuses on creating the conditions for people and teams to thrive. It is about building trust, fostering creativity, and empowering people to take ownership of their work. Generative leaders are also able to adapt to change and learn from failure.

Generative leadership is essential for success in the Fourth and Next Industrial Revolutions. Organizations need to innovate quickly and respond to change effectively in this new era. Generative leaders can create the conditions for this by building a culture of learning, collaboration, and trust.

Beyond The Windowsill

In the sequel of the Ashanti MWendo series, we embark on a captivating journey with Ashanti as she navigates the complexities of leading two tech giants, Avant-Garde Metaverse (AGM) and Uwazi, while balancing the demands of motherhood and partnership.

The tapestry of Ashanti's life is richly woven with diverse threads, each essential to her life's journey. Her husband, Ayo, and twin 12-year-old children, Carmel and Caleb, who live on the spectrum with exceptional gifts, provide her with a steadfast anchor of love and support.

As Ashanti spearheads AGM's product development and Uwazi's interim CEO, she must masterfully balance her dual roles, harnessing her agility and vision to spur continuous innovation in both realms. The dynamic world of Uwazi, a nascent venture poised to amplify its Metaverse offerings through the innovative use of AI deepfakes and security tokens, presents Ashanti with new challenges and opportunities.

This captivating sequel will witness Ashanti's unwavering commitment to her family, career, and passion for innovation. We will cheer her on as she overcomes obstacles and achieves new heights, blazing a trail for other women, men, girls, boys, and 'they' to follow.

The Innovation Catalyst, Leading With Empathy,

We follow the inspiring journey of Ashanti MWendo as she takes on her new role as Chief Product Officer at Avante Garde Virtual Reality. Amidst a world of mediocre customer sentiment and outdated technology platforms, Ashanti must confront the challenge of revitalizing the company's once-popular fantasy vacation VR product, which has been plagued by motion sickness issues.

As the metaverse revolution looms on the horizon, Ashanti's determination and leadership are put to the test. With the company's future at stake, she embarks on an ambitious quest to transform the underperforming VR product and nurture a culture of innovation within Avante Garde. By championing an entrepreneurship program for internal employees and community partners, Ashanti seeks to unleash the untapped potential of her team.

Ashanti's journey is a gripping tale of perseverance and triumph in the face of adversity. Through Ashanti's visionary leadership, we explore the importance of embracing change, fostering creativity, and empowering individuals to make a lasting impact on the ever-evolving metaverse world of virtual reality. This powerful narrative serves as a reminder that when faced with seemingly insurmountable obstacles, the human spirit is capable of achieving extraordinary feats.

Deliver Value: Happy Contributing People, Satisfied Customers, And Thriving Business

Deliver Value by Dr. Dave A. Cornelius presents a groundbreaking framework for understanding what it truly means to create value for people, organizations, and society, especially in the twenty-first century. People often think they understand the concept of value until they're challenged to explain it to someone else.

In the book, Dr. Dave focuses on navigating innovation in an environment that is volatile, uncertain, complex, and ambiguous (VUCA). The author uses both fictitious short stories and real-life examples to help readers and listeners relate to various paths of producing value. These stories help describe what providing value in the real world looks like. In addition, the author offers excerpts from interviews with four company executives to offer concrete illustrations of what value looks like in today's unpredictable, complicated, and confusing environment.

Belonging And Healing: Creating Awareness For Yourself And Others

Belonging and Healing by Dr. Dave A. Cornelius revolves around the central theme of creating awesomeness for yourself and others in an organization. To do this, everyone must feel like they belong, and wounds must be healed. The path to healing and belonging calls for reflection and exploration to evolve. He addresses individuals and organizations involved in professional coaching, corporate coaching, and DEI. However, other professionals may use the ideas and methods to enhance a sense of connection and healing in collectives.

Elastic Minds: What Are You Thinking?

Elastic minds are creatives who reimagine ways to create businesses, define how people engage in learning, and create tools to change markets. People who can think elastically produce game-changing outcomes that are available globally. Each chapter includes the stories of several small business owners and leaders striving to achieve goals and sustain the American dream of being self-determined.

- In the chapter titled "The Power of Observation", Tracy Treacy's leadership profile describes her journey as a private practice Therapist.
- Dr. Dave Martinez's leadership profile highlights his journey as a high school principal in the "Continual Learning" chapter.
- Kevin Castle, the Managing Director of a technology consulting business, is profiled in the "Climbing the Mountains – Clearing the Hurdles" chapter.

- In the chapter "The Story of Getting There", Tammy Hawkins, Managing Director at Experis, tells her story.
- Richard Dolman, Vice President at Agile42, gives insights into his leadership experience in the "Smaller and More Frequent Delivery" chapter.
- Alicia McLain, Business owner of Operational Innovations, highlights her growth as a leader in the "Learn fast – Inspect and Adapt" chapter.
- In the chapter "You don't know it until you do it", Jill Freeman Stack, Principal at Jill Stack PR, gives her testimony of her career growth into business ownership.
- Agile Marketing Coach James Wright tells his triumph story in the "Check the Rearview Mirror" chapter.
- In the chapter "Pay it Forward for Those Who Follow", Wes Kliewer, Director of Learning at Project Insights, tells his story.
- Bobby Cooper Jr. Owner of El Cheapo Lift share his powerful moments of courage in the "When You Fall Stand Again" chapter.

My hope is for you to exercise your elastic mind and find what is your motivation and purpose in life.

Prayers To My Abba Father God,

Prayer is asking, expecting, receiving, and responding based on frequent conversations with our Abba Father God. We engage in intimate discussions as often as needed to help with the journey through each day. The prayers included in this book began as songs intended to be recorded for worship. However, prayer is one way to worship and celebrate the goodness we have received and the corrections to help us grow. The prayers written in this book are categorized into three themes: 1) gratitude, 2) wandering, and 3) being still. A life filled with gratitude demonstrates being content with the gifts received in life, no matter how small. We wonder physically, mentally, emotionally, and spiritually. Think of the Israelites in the Old Testament, wandering the desert for 40 years. According to historical facts, the journey should have only taken 11 days to reach the promised land from Egypt to Canaan. When we take time to be still, it acknowledges the goodness of being in God's rest.

The book of Psalms contains many songs of praise that many people read daily for guidance. I invite you to read these prayers to help you create your own prayers. God loves creative people! That is why God set aside the Levites as a unique group of people responsible for music. I invite musicians to take these words, add melodies, make new chord changes, and share them with the world.

Transforming Your Leadership Character: The Lean Thinking And Agility Way.

People need better leaders to guide them, but they also desire to become better leaders themselves, both at home and at work. People strive to be the best leaders in many aspects of life, including businesses, churches, non-profits, sports teams, and more.

Corporate professionals and other practitioners in various disciplines aim to be solid leaders. But despite training and mentoring, people still fall short of becoming leaders who inspire others to deliver to the best of their abilities. We all have leadership traits based on experience and observation, but proactive efforts are needed to grow and transform these skills. The appropriate level of planning, nurturing, and execution can help leaders navigate the course from a non-starter to a resilient starter and finisher.

Shawn, Chase, and Mario are three personas that represent the leadership dispositions of resilient, quick, and non-starters and finishers. They model how to use lean thinking and agility to transform your leadership character.

Seven Principles And Habits For Kingdom Living. A Guide For Your Past, Present, And Future Life.

What if Kingdom Living gained popularity? I'm not talking about a fleeting trend but a transformation that resonates with people worldwide. Individuals would prioritize living with purpose and integrity, striving to reflect in every aspect of their lives the examples set by Christ Jesus. Communities would become beacons of unity and cooperation, with neighbors supporting one another and pooling resources to meet shared needs.

I want to maximize my free will to experience Kingdom Living every day. My goal is to minimize mistakes and poor choices while enhancing the quality of my living experiences with family, friends, and community. The seven Kingdom principles and habits that guide my spiritual life include:

1. Principle One: Love God, Yourself, and Your Neighbor.
2. Principle Two: Be Holy.
3. Principle Three: Store up treasures in heaven for yourself.
4. Principle Four: Give generously with your heart.
5. Principle Five: Live by the Spirit of God.
6. Principle Six: Live debt-free.
7. Principle Seven: Leave an inheritance for your children's children.

"I invite you to journey through this book with an open heart and mind, ready to be transformed. Let the principles contained herein be not only read but also lived. As Dr. Dave beautifully puts it, these teachings are not just for knowing but for doing. Prepare to be challenged, inspired, and changed." -- Demetrius Miles, Lead Pastor; The Gathering at Tucson

"If you've drifted away from God, the seven principles outlined in this book will help you find your way back. When I was asked to read and write the foreword for this book, I encountered a series of distractions that tried to keep me from reading it. Now I understand why this book is truly life-changing." -- Minister Sheree Carradine

"Dr. Dave's seven principles and habits are simple, which is what Jesus Christ stands for—simplicity, sacrifice, and salvation. This book is practical! Dr. Dave describes the WHAT of each principle and HOW it can be applied in daily life in the home and the marketplace. This helps close most Christians' gap between their 'spiritual life' and 'marketplace life,' when there should not be any difference." -- Temitope Bolaji-Jegede